▶ **Affective Disorder and the Writing Life**

Other Palgrave Pivot titles

Michael J. Osborne: **Multiple Interest Rate Analysis: Theory and Applications**

Barry Stocker: **Kierkegaard on Politics**

Lauri Rapeli: **The Conception of Citizen Knowledge in Democratic Theory**

Michele Acuto and Simon Curtis: **Reassembling International Theory: Assemblage Thinking and International Relations**

Stephan Klingebiel: **Development Cooperation: Challenges of the New Aid Architecture**

Mia Moody-Ramirez and Jannette Dates: **The Obamas and Mass Media: Race, Gender, Religion, and Politics**

Kenneth Weisbrode: **Old Diplomacy Revisited**

Christopher Mitchell: **Decentralization and Party Politics in the Dominican Republic**

Keely Byars-Nichols: **The Black Indian in American Literature**

Vincent P. Barabba: **Business Strategies for a Messy World: Tools for Systemic Problem-Solving**

Cristina Archetti: **Politicians, Personal Image and the Construction of Political Identity: A Comparative Study of the UK and Italy**

Mitchell Congram, Peter Bell and Mark Lauchs: **Policing Transnational Organised Crime and Corruption: Exploring Communication Interception Technology**

János Kelemen: **The Rationalism of Georg Lukács**

Patrick Manning: **Big Data in History**

Susan D. Rose: **Challenging Global Gender Violence: The Global Clothesline Project**

Thomas Janoski: **Dominant Divisions of Labor: Models of Production That Have Transformed the World of Work**

Gray Read: **Modern Architecture in Theater: The Experiments of Art et Action**

Bill Lucarelli: **Endgame for the Euro: A Critical Theory**

Robert Frodeman: **Sustainable Knowledge: A Theory of Interdisciplinarity**

Antonio V. Menéndez Alarcón: **French and US Approaches to Foreign Policy**

Stephen Turner: **American Sociology: From Pre-Disciplinary to Post-Normal**

Ekaterina Dorodnykh: **Stock Market Integration: An International Perspective**

Bill Lucarelli: **Endgame for the Euro: A Critical History**

Mercedes Bunz: **The Silent Revolution: How Digitalization Transforms Knowledge, Work, Journalism and Politics without Making Too Much Noise**

Kishan S. Rana: **The Contemporary Embassy: Paths to Diplomatic Excellence**

Mark Bracher: **Educating for Cosmopolitanism: Lessons from Cognitive Science and Literature**

Carroll P. Kakel, III: **The Holocaust as Colonial Genocide: Hitler's 'Indian Wars' in the 'Wild East'**

Laura Linker: **Lucretian Thought in Late Stuart England: Debates about the Nature of the Soul**

DOI: 10.1057/9781137381668

palgrave▶pivot

Affective Disorder and the Writing Life: The Melancholic Muse

Edited by

Stephanie Stone Horton
Teaching Assistant, Georgia State University, USA

Selection and editorial content © Stephanie Stone Horton 2014
Individual chapters © the contributors 2014
Foreword © Marya Hornbacher 2014

All rights reserved. No reproduction, copy or transmission of this publication may be made without written permission.

No portion of this publication may be reproduced, copied or transmitted save with written permission or in accordance with the provisions of the Copyright, Designs and Patents Act 1988, or under the terms of any licence permitting limited copying issued by the Copyright Licensing Agency, Saffron House, 6–10 Kirby Street, London EC1N 8TS.

Any person who does any unauthorized act in relation to this publication may be liable to criminal prosecution and civil claims for damages.

The authors have asserted their rights to be identified as the author of this work in accordance with the Copyright, Designs and Patents Act 1988.

First published 2014 by
PALGRAVE MACMILLAN

Palgrave Macmillan in the UK is an imprint of Macmillan Publishers Limited, registered in England, company number 785998, of Houndmills, Basingstoke, Hampshire RG21 6XS.

Palgrave Macmillan in the US is a division of St Martin's Press LLC, 175 Fifth Avenue, New York, NY 10010.

Palgrave Macmillan is the global academic imprint of the above companies and has companies and representatives throughout the world.

Palgrave® and Macmillan® are registered trademarks in the United States, the United Kingdom, Europe and other countries.

ISBN: 978–1–137–38167–5 EPUB
ISBN: 978–1–137–38166–8 PDF
ISBN: 978–1–137–38165–1 Hardback

A catalogue record for this book is available from the British Library.

A catalog record for this book is available from the Library of Congress.

www.palgrave.com/pivot

DOI: 10.1057/9781137381668

For John, Grace, and Lynée

Contents

Foreword by Marya Hornbacher	viii
Notes on Contributors	xii

Part I   "Could It Be Madness, This?" Affective Difference and the Work of Composition

1	"What Ceremony of Words Can Patch the Havoc?": Composition and Madness *Stephanie Stone Horton*	2
2	Muse Afire: Negotiating the Line between Creative Pursuit and Mental Illness *Nancer Ballard*	24
3	After the Fire Goes Out: Writing before and after Treatment for an Affective Disorder *Lise Bagoley*	43
4	Gaps on the Vita *Sharon O'Brien*	55
5	Lunatic *Jeannie Parker Beard*	69

Part II   "Their Lives a Storm Whereon They Ride": Affective (Dis)order and the Literary Imagination

6	Axing the Frozen Sea: Female Inscriptions of Madness *Joann K. Deiudicibus*	79

7 The Things We Carry: Embodied Truth and
   Tim O' Brien's Poetics of Despair   100
   David Bahr

8 "The Incessant Rise and Fall and Fall and Rise":
   Virginia Woolf Treading the Waves   116
   Jessica De Santa

9 The Fire, the Dark, and the Beautiful Distance   129
   Stephen Newton

Index   141

Foreword

Rarely are writers so tempted to write upon a thing as they are to write upon writing, which is more than a little mimetic, but becomes even more so when they are specifically writing about the process of writing – when writers write on the writing mind.

It's necessarily a muddled process, from an academic and literary project of major mental acrobatics to a philosophical conundrum from which the writerly human animal cannot be released.

▶ This book explores the shape and nature of the place wherein the disorderly mind meets up and merges with the orderly structures of language and form; the shadowed space wherein the writer's perception bleeds into and becomes the writer's work; and the process of writing itself.

The urge toward language, toward a structure of words that can order and express the miasma of feeling and thought that swirls within what we know as the self, is one of our most basic human needs. It isn't a need specific to a kind of mind; it is an urge that flows through our bones regardless of where we may fall (at any given moment) on the spectrum between orderly and disorderly moods and minds. This collection explores, then, not only the direct influence of affective disorder on writing, but the way in which writing is an expression of the collective human need to shape experience, to share it – to speak. The act of writing is a literalization of the writing mind. It is the hand sketching the mind, or it's the hand sketching itself, sketching and erasing itself as it goes, scrawling and disappearing in the selfsame act. It is like writing in sand except it's not; it's more like writing in water. A tiny flurry of shapes ripples past as the hand writes its name, leaving only the shimmering skin of the water in its wake.

Which is not to say that writing about writing is solipsistic – I don't believe that it is. I believe the urge to investigate the mind with the mind, to explore the creative act by the creative act, is both natural and necessary.

We write ourselves alive, we write ourselves to sleep, we write ourselves to visibility and then to invisibility again. We come and we go in an instant. Our stories, though, remain. I do not think we tell our stories for ourselves. We tell our stories for the Other, that someone, that reader, that second person, that You. E.M. Forster gives the directive that every writer ultimately obeys: "Only connect." By telling stories, we do.

These studies cut away the dross of the madness mythos to show how these writers and others are driven ultimately not by chemistry or illness but by what Joann K. Deiudicibus aptly describes as the "human compulsion to make and share meaning".

And who can better describe the process of meaning-making than those who use words often and well? And who are the people who walk the terra infirma of creativity, the shifting sand where mood and mind, emotion and thought, feeling and fact, intersect, than people who ride the swells and falls of the moody mind? The people who necessarily must examine, and must seek to understand, the activity of their minds for their very survival – and can, as a result, tell others how the mind acts on them, speaks through them, and makes meaning from them?

As Nancer Ballard writes, her project – and I would say a clear goal of this collection – is to speak to "all who've struggled to make the trip through darkness, or sought to create something from nothing". The process of creative work – to seek to create something from nothing – cannot help but exist in that ephemeral place where mind and mood wend their way around one another's feet. Those who have personal experience with affective disorders know well how the activity of mind is forever inflected by the mood, and any writer who's ever tried to write, or write well, knows how their mood is inflected by the activities of their mind. (I once memorably read about the writing process as "trying to bleed through one's forehead by force of will", which is very apt, I think, and describes the messy, absurdist process of trying to capture a tangible world that we perceive as a sensate onslaught of image and object in a carefully woven but ultimately insubstantial net of words. A silly project, frankly. But we can't help it. We can't help but translate our world into the inchoate babble of the languages we know.)

The language we have for the disordered mind is limited at best, as it must be: we are never pure mind, but always mind and mood, emotion and thought, body and brain being one and the same. We may call a disruption in that continuum "mental illness", but that does not describe the experience of being pushed and pulled by the riptide of selves, by the multitudes that Whitman claims we contain. I choose the word "madness" instead.

"Madness" carries within it several meanings at once: Its two syllables speak to the historical notions of the mentally ill person (as divinely inspired madman, as madwoman in the attic, as melancholic Romantic, as self-destructive romantic, and so forth). The word echoes with the artistic or literary idea of Madness, which still holds a sway in our collective unconscious as inherent to the artist, a fallacy that too often glorifies the self-annihilating impulse that exists in most persons, or any other thing capable of contemplating its own being or unbeing. And the word speaks, however inexactly, to the lived experience of having what we know as mental illness. The word holds the crosscurrent that is not specific to the "ill", but instead is the complex experience of internal disorder that strains to order its selves, its perceptions, its worlds.

How does this confluence of meanings inflect the writing practice and the writer's life? How does the idea of madness shape the social understanding of writers and other artists, or of creativity itself? And, perhaps most importantly, how does the presence of madness influence – if it does – the reader's experience of the words? What is the relationship between the reader and a work written by someone who is "mad"? Is there a relationship at all? Or does the work exist unto itself? No creative process or product exists in a vacuum, outside of society – but does the work stand on its own, apart from its writer, apart from the singular self, emerging from my mind and entering yours?

These pieces work together not only to understand the connection between an inner experience of disorder and the act of writing toward order again, but also to map the spot where writer and reader intersect (at points X and Y, which we shall call the heart and mind). As intellectual historiography and literary analysis, such a collection would be incomplete without examinations of writers who have significantly influenced the use of language and the expression of mind. Jessica De Santa examines with precision the explicit and implicit manifestations of madness in Virginia Woolf's prose; Joann K. Deiudicibus explores the way Anne Sexton's poetry performs a kind of alchemy by which the writer achieves both order and voice.

And this book could not function without examinations of the relationship of the writing process to the written work by people who deal with affective disorders themselves. David Bahr reads Tim O'Brien's "The Things They Carried" as an "aesthetic autobiography" that finds in the borderland between fact and fiction a testament to "the power of story to affectively connect people". Sharon O'Brien addresses the struggle to maintain literary productivity while living with depression, speaking to the conflict between the linear, hierarchical demands of the academy and the cyclical, inescapable demands of the affectively disordered mind.

Each chapter, though variant in voice and tone from each to each, is a critical part of the whole, and the whole here may be defined as the sometimes flowing, sometimes unsteady scrawl of the disorderly writing mind. Readers may disagree with points of view, some or all; they may find it unsettling or problematic to see the inclusion of literary voices in an academic work, or academic voices in a literary work, or first-person narratives in anything, but they will find the writing skilled and often thrilling, and the intellectual caliber high. This is not a book about writing for writers, or a book about mental illness for people who have it, or an esoteric undertaking of vague concepts for the purpose of everyone's vitae. It is a book that engages writers and readers in a dialectic on the way we think, feel, and write our way through the clutter of self and life, and arrive on the other side with a story that speaks to the larger culture and world.

These chapters bring to mind words of Adrienne Rich: "The words are purposes. / The words are maps. / I came to see the damage that was done/and the treasures that prevail". The authors gathered here describe the downward swim into the inchoate waters of the human mind, the discoveries they make in the deep, and the surge upward again. What they bring to us are the glinting insights they find.

Marya Hornbacher

Notes on Contributors

"**Lise Bagoley**" is the pen name of a writer who is an Assistant Visiting Professor of English at a private Eastern university, where she teaches both literature and composition. She holds a PhD and MA in English, and minored in creative writing as an undergraduate. Her primary research focus is contemporary American literature and films set in the suburbs; she also has a strong interest in creative writing and the intersections of health, medicine, and literature. She was diagnosed with bipolar disorder in her mid-twenties.

David Bahr is Assistant Professor of English at the Borough of Manhattan Community College, The City University of New York. He received his doctorate in postwar twentieth-century American literature and autobiography at The Graduate Center of The City University of New York. His journalism and creative writing have appeared in numerous publications, including *The New York Times*, *The New York Times Book Review*, *GQ*, *Poets & Writers*, *Publishers Weekly*, *The Village Voice*, *Prairie Schooner*, *Time Out New York*, *The Advocate*, *Out*, *Spin*, *Reconstruction: Studies in Contemporary Culture*, and the anthology *Boys to Men: Gay Men Write about Growing Up*. His work has been cited by *The Best American Essays* series and *The Missouri Review*, and he has been awarded writing fellowships at Yaddo and The Edward Albee Foundation.

Nancer Ballard is a fiction and nonfiction writer, poet, lawyer, and a Resident Scholar at Brandeis University's Women's Studies Research Center. She is the author of *Dead Reckoning* and a co-author of a supplemental children's textbook series that teaches mathematics though multicultural based story telling. Recent works appeared in *Thema Literary Journal, Frostwriting, Unlocking the Poem*, and an essay on time in narrative nonfiction is forthcoming in *The Far Reaches of the Fourth Genre*. She is currently working on a memoir incorporating history, psychology, and neurobiology entitled *The Odd Direction of Heaven*.

Jessica De Santa is a fourth-year PhD candidate at the University of St Andrews in Scotland. She researches food and taste in the novels and essays of Virginia Woolf and French writer Hélène Cixous. She has received her master's in Women, Writing, and Gender from St Andrews. In addition to her doctoral research, Jessica teaches literature and writing in New Jersey, her home state. She has previously worked as a cookbook editor and a piano salesperson.

Joann K. Deiudicibus is the Staff Assistant for the Composition Program and an Adjunct Instructor at The State University of New York, New Paltz, where she earned her MA in English (2003). Her interests include cats, creativity, and mental illness, and twentieth-century American poetry, particularly the work of Anne Sexton. She is the Associate Editor (poetry) for Laurence Carr's *WaterWrites: A Hudson River Anthology*. Her poetry was selected for the Woodstock Poetry Festival (2003) and has appeared in *The North Street Journal, The Orange Review, Literary Passions, Fortunate Fall, Chronogram, The Shawangunk Review*, and will appear in the forthcoming collection *A Slant of Light: Contemporary Women Writers of the Hudson Valley*.

Stephanie Stone Horton is a fourth-year PhD student in Rhetoric and Composition at Georgia State University. She is a Phi Beta Kappa journalism graduate of the University of Oklahoma, with an MA in American Literature from the University of North Texas. She has worked as a journalist and was accepted into two law schools, but thought twice. Her scholarly interests include composition and the affective disorders; neurodiversity and disability studies; rhetorics of emotion as social, embodied, and shared; advertising and consumer culture; Internet behavioral advertising and privacy; critical pedagogy; and the disciplinary history of composition studies. Stephanie lives and writes with bipolar disorder.

Sharon O'Brien, a former Fulbright scholar, has written two critical biographies of Willa Cather, including *Willa Cather: The Emerging Voice*. Her more recent publications include *The Family Silver: A Memoir of Depression* *and Inheritance*. O'Brien also writes short stories and personal essays. She teaches interdisciplinary, English and American studies at Dickinson College, and her teaching and research interests include the politics of memory, illness and narrative, and lifewriting. She quotes Cather, who was fond of saying "The journey – not the arrival – matters."

Stephen Newton is Associate Professor of English at William Paterson University in Wayne, New Jersey. He was a Fulbright Scholar in 2005–2006 at the Institute for American Studies at the University of Graz in Austria. As a younger man he pumped gas in Alamosa, Colorado, drove a forklift at a cement factory in Cleveland, was a nightshift janitor at the Grand Ole Opry, and one memorable Christmas was Santa Claus in a shopping mall outside Nashville.

Jeannie Parker Beard is a lover of life, imagination, and creativity. She lives in the North Georgia mountains with her adventurous husband and adorable son. She believes in the power of intention and the value of education. She writes, teaches, and imagines how we can make the world a better place through love and appreciation of the things that we don't always understand. Her family is inspiration for most of her musings and contemplations, and she is sure that experience brings wisdom. She has a PhD in rhetoric and composition from Georgia State University.

Part I
"Could It Be Madness, This?" Affective Difference and the Work of Composition

▶

1
"What Ceremony of Words Can Patch the Havoc?": Composition and Madness

Stephanie Stone Horton

Abstract: *In a 15-year longitudinal study little known outside of psychiatry, fully 80 per cent of a writers' group at the Iowa Writers' Workshop reported living with, or experiencing an incidence of, an affective disorder – as opposed to 30 per cent of non-writer controls. Springing from this study, this survey breaks ground by examining the persistent linkage of affective disorders (depression and bipolar disorder) and writing creativity, from the* Phaedrus *to today's stunning PET and SPECT scans of depressed, manic, and non-affectively disordered brains. The essay also calls for new research alliances between composition studies and neuroscience – research into states such as writer's block, hypergraphia, and the exuberant pressured speech of mania. The year 2013 marks the fiftieth anniversary of Sylvia Plath's suicide; her work provides fertile ground for this exploration of affective madness and invention.*

Keywords: Affective disorders; creativity; depression; bipolar disorder; writer's block; hypergraphia; neuroscience; Sylvia Plath

Horton, Stephanie Stone, ed. *Affective Disorder and the Writing Life: The Melancholic Muse*. Basingstoke: Palgrave Macmillan, 2014. DOI: 10.1057/9781137381668.

Cutting through

> To be a poet is a condition, not a profession.
>
> Robert Greaves
>
> Of all that is written I love only what a man has written with his blood.
>
> Nietzsche

First day of a graduate class, and we must create a metaphor for our own writing. A free write-and-share, a little harmless fun.

A 30-year-old memory flows in, unstoppable. An Oklahoma sky so blue it hurts. Red blood on gray pavement. I put pen to paper, and the chorus – a familiar presence – sidles up, taking my elbow.

> "What on earth – you can't write that!" it whispers.

The room is quiet, save for scribbling. My knot-heart turns to stone. Now that I think of it, this metaphor is bizarre; I have no idea where it is trying to go. I try to think of another, but this unwanted child of the mind crowds out all others. The chorus weighs in again, oracular:

> This metaphor has nothing to do with writing! It's gratuitous. These people are going to think you're a freak.

The *minutes* tick by. I cast a furtive glance at the writer on my left ("For me, writing is like cooking") and the notebook on my right ("For me, writing is like gardening"). Both knowledgeable, *ethos* appropriate to audience. My throat closes. Once again, I try – hard – to commit even a single word to paper, to capture sky and wind and horror. Now the chorus gets personal:

> You just want attention, don't you? You're pathologically morbid. You're already an outsider here; this little trick will cement it.

Out of time and ideas, I force metaphor to paper:

For me, writing is like opening a vein. Mind you, I've never actually opened a vein. But that's how it feels when I try to write. I'm not a cutter, but I know they find relief in the cutting through of things, in the warm living flow.

When I was 19, I saw a girl die in a motorcycle accident. A station wagon ran a stop sign and broadsided the bike and its two riders, who flew over the car like rag dolls. One tried to get up despite an ankle snapped 90 degrees. The other landed on her head, and was utterly still.

A passing nurse began CPR. A halo of dark red blood fanned on the pavement around the girl's helmet. I couldn't help her, but I couldn't leave her, either. The frantic lifesavers began to sound far away.

That's when I noticed it, from a place beside myself. Her blood was clotting, there on the street. All of it. Hundreds of little clumps forming on the smooth gray pavement. The girl was dead, but the blood language was alive – a consciousness of its own, a last beautiful grasping at life.

I don't like to bleed. That's why it's hard for me to write. I want to stay whole and safe and keep my words in. Once spilled, my words take on a life of their own.

I read first, and for a long moment, there was silence. "Well", said the gardener. "I hate to follow that."

My writing was not rejected – far from it. The blessing of strangers allows me to exhale. Yet physiologically, I remain poised for imminent conflict, adrenals surging with cortisol, stone heart pounding. I feel devastated. Listening to the other students read, I slowly begin to calm, and realize I had cut through to something vital. This long-ago scene helped me understand the pain behind my writing – the lifeblood, the broken body, the communion with audience, the cutting through that is the job of every writer.

Much of the time, however, I can't cut through.

On writing and depression

> [We] must understand [madness] not as reason diseased, or as reason lost or alienated, but quite simply as reason dazzled.
>
> Foucault, Madness and Civilization (108)

> I owe a supreme, metaphysical lucidity to my depression…. Sometimes, I have the arrogant feeling of being witness to the meaninglessness of Being…. My pain is the hidden side of my philosophy, its mute sister.
>
> Julia Kristeva, Black Sun: Depression and Melancholia (4)

This chapter, the one you're reading, is way past deadline – a casual deadline, but a deadline still. My mentor, a scholar of great energy and wit, a veritable publishing machine – is through with me. Friends claim that no evidence exists for this, but I know it at the deepest levels. My amygdalae – deep-brain, almond-shaped structures, the diminutive portrait artists of the human brain, our readers of human faces – have registered a furrow in her brow, instantly obliterating a thousand smiles.

With a predictability verging on the comic, my ornate and lengthy Scroll of Professional Failures unfurls – but not before I manage one moment of clarity: These despairing thoughts, these visions of failure, these distortions of memory, are madness – the depressive phase of manic–depression.

I live and write with manic–depression (I prefer this older, more descriptive term, rather than the vague "bipolar"). Yet I am a walking binary, deconstructed daily by this disease of perception. Manic–depression occurs in roughly 2.6 per cent of the American population. Nine per cent of American adults experience major unipolar depression in a given year, and half of those meet criteria for severe depression (CDC 2013). According to the World Health Organization, depression is the leading cause of disability worldwide, affecting 350 million people (WHO 2012). Ten per cent of American undergraduates seek treatment for it during any given year and seven per cent take antidepressants (ACHA 2012). It is naive to think affective difference has nothing to do with writing. Yet until very recently, the phenomenon has received only spotty attention from rhetoric and composition studies.

Long-term studies show that the affective disorders (depression and manic–depressive illness) are far overrepresented in writers. One compilation, "Suicide Rates in Writers and Artists" (Jamison 1989), yields startling data:

> Expected rate of suicide in the general population: less than one per cent. Expected rate of suicide, all writers: seven per cent (Andreasen 1987) Rate of suicide in poets: 18 per cent. (Ludwig 1992, working from 30 years of biographical studies from 1000 eminent individuals, including poets). Poets had highest rate of depression of all professions. (Jamison 89)

The suicide rate for female poets is highest of all; one psychiatric researcher has dubbed this "the Sylvia Plath effect" (Kaufman 37). Theories and etiologies of depressive disorder abound, but one study suggests that depressed women may be more likely to use rumination – a profoundly isolating activity – as a form of emotional regulation (272). I am a writer who ruminates. I mull over and over my mentor's brow; actual discourse with her is, as Robert Lowell described manic–depression, "seeing too much and feeling it/with one skin layer missing" (Goodwin and Jamison 341). In my pain, I've often wondered: Why do these disorders exist? Why haven't they cycled out of the gene pool? And why do they carry strong links to artistic endeavor? Jonah Lehrer,

DOI: 10.1057/9781137381668

writing in *The New York Times*, suggests that the Pleistocene hunter-gatherer didn't have much time for self-loathing; he or she probably didn't undergo paroxysms of shame over a dumb comment in a faculty meeting. Lehrer theorizes that rumination seems to be intertwined with an obsessive cognitive style that may facilitate the production of art. Inch by inch, it extends a taproot, a deeper vision.

Depression and bipolar illness are among the most painful of human maladies, saboteurs of the delicate machinery of sleep, emotion, cognition, and perception. The semantic shift from "melancholy" to "depression" wove its way into collective discourse around 1912, the brainchild of Johns Hopkins psychiatrist Louis Meyer, the same fellow who gave us "mental hygiene". Meyer invented "depression" to supplant the rich, millennia-old melancholy – the melan (black) chole (bile) of Hippocrates, Arteus, and Galen. In the bloodless language of psychiatry, depression involves, among other things, a dysregulation of the limbic/hypothalamic/pituitary axis; it is a neurochemical symphony far out of tune. The novelist William Styron, in *Darkness Visible: A Memoir of Madness*, decried the gross linguistic inadequacy of the word "depression" (47). What Styron described was agony beyond agony, of "slowed-down responses, near paralysis, psychic energy throttled back to zero" (47). Styron describes suicidal depression as "a fiercely overheated room with no exits... the rational mind begins to seek oblivion" (47).

Melancholy has compelled as far back as Aristotle, who famously asked:

> Why is it that all men who are outstanding in philosophy, poetry or the arts are melancholic? The same is true of Ajax and Bellerophontes... and many other heroes suffered in the same way as these. In later times also there have been Empedocles, Plato, Socrates and many other well-known men. The same is true of most of those who have handled poetry. (*Problemata*)

Writers (Byron 1853) have been drawn to the associative fluidity and creative zeal associated with some states of hypomania and mania; presumably, they do not bargain for the murky, death-obsessed, neurological hell of severe depression, that dark anarchy of the psyche, in which a writer's "breath is agitation, and their lives/A storm whereon they ride" (136).

In a longitudinal study spanning 15 years, psychiatric researcher Nancy Andreasen followed 30 writers at the Iowa Writers' Workshop, publishing data in *The American Journal of Psychiatry* (1987). Andreasen had hypothesized a link between schizophrenia and creative writing, but

15 years of data revealed not a single case of schizophrenia among the writers. What *did* capture the researchers' attention: *80 per cent* of the Iowa writers reported living with, or a lifetime incidence of, an affective disorder (mainly bipolar illness), while affective disorders were indicated in only *30 per cent* of controls (non-writers matched for age, sex, and educational level, hailing from careers like insurance and banking). Even the first-degree relatives of the Iowa writers were, in Andreasen's words, "riddled with creativity and mental illness", with these traits only "randomly scattered" among relatives of controls (1292). Two of the Iowa writers committed suicide during the term of study; statistics show that nearly one in five persons with bipolar disorder will end life in suicide, so painful is the malady (Jamison 41). Throughout the 15-year study (Andreasen and Glick 1988), the Iowa writers "consistently reported they were unable to write during periods of depression"; they also described writing produced in mania as "disjointed and often of poor quality" (212). Severe depression and mania – intensely painful and debilitating – do not lend themselves to writing; mild depression and hypomania (mild mania) seem to hold the key. For the Iowa writers, affective disorders are both "a hereditary taint, and a hereditary gift" (Andreasen 1282).

Increasingly, neuroscience research is focusing on language and writing:

1 Depressed subjects showed "clear deficits" in memory, global verbal learning ability, recall of positive memories, ideational flexibility, and the ability to recall the "gist" of a story (Turnera et al. 2012).
2 Original, creative responses to a word-association test increase threefold in mania, whereas the number of predictable responses falls by a third (Pons et al.).
3 Depression increases rumination, memory of negative stimuli, cognitive distortions, cognitive biases, inferior memory strategies, attention deficits, and decreases in executive functioning (Moffit et al. 1994, Thomas et al. 2007, Murrough et al. 2011). The writing of depressed eminent writers contains "significantly more cognitive distortions" than the writing of eminent non-depressed writers (Thomas et al. 2007).
4 Depression increases use of the first person, intransitive verbs, and passive voice (Stirman and Pennebaker 2001).
5 Bipolar writers refer to death more often, and to other people less often, than depressed and control writers (Forgeard 2008).

Engaging with rhetorics of neuroscience would open new discourse into writing. Rosemarie Garland-Thompson, writing in disability studies, calls disabled bodies "extraordinary bodies". I propose we think in terms of "extraordinary brains", extraordinary in part because of pathology. James Kaufman found that writers who had reached a pinnacle of achievement, such as the Pulitzer or Nobel Prize, were more likely to suffer from mental illness than other writers (2001).

Academics rarely "come out" with an affective disorder. Katie Rose Guest Pryal has identified rhetorical strategies employed by mood memoirs (for instance, Lauren Slater's *Prozac Diary*); these restorative strategies include "laying claim", or listing famous or accomplished people with the disorder. The impulse is understandable: We lose rhetorical agency when we identify as mentally ill; our ethos incurs damage from which it will never fully recover. For Emily Martin, the performative act of diagnosis creates a circular trap; we are forever assigned to "the subject position of the irrational" (128). I compare disclosure to the purchase of a new Jaguar; the moment it rolls off the lot, its value decreases by half, with the promise of much maintenance ahead. Yet, a metastudy conducted at the Tufts University School of Medicine examined 81 studies and articles on people with bipolar disorder, and identified 5 positive psychological traits, including spirituality, empathy, creativity, realism, and resilience (Galvez et al.).

In the two and a half millennia since the *Phaedrus*, the *locus classicus* of madness and the writer's art, the "mad writer" has become *nomos*, alternately romanticized and stigmatized, a rich vein waiting to be unearthed by scholars of rhetoric, composition, and literature. Of course, any inquiry into intersections of madness and art raises scores of questions, of methodology, historiography, ethics, psychiatry, psychopharmacology, criticism, and the enduring question: Who or what defines mental illness, and how? Composition scholars have long overlooked potential conversations between composition studies and rhetorics of psychiatry and mental illness. Typically, it is "pathologizing" to suggest that the act of writing involves both a body and a brain; only in "the affective turn" of the last 20 years, through the work of feminist critics like Laura Micciche, have affect and reason even been recognized as a double helix rather than a binary, with two millennia of the privileging of reason. To ignore emotion is to ignore half of ourselves. In Micciche's work, emotions are "the heart of rhetoric"; they are "what makes meanings stick" (7). Our affective lives are dynamically rhetorical; the brain's affective networks drive "the continual repositioning of ourselves in the face of ever-changing situations" (3). Yet for Richard Vatz, writing in the *Encyclopedia of Rhetoric and Composition,* psychiatry is "one of the least examined and most effective rhetorical systems in existence" (Enos 615). In criticism, the interrogation of pathological processes of mental illness is considered essentialist, mechanistic, and reductive. Indeed, it has become "positivist and naive and to acknowledge affective difference at all" (Kantor 31).

In the next century, neuroscience promises to do for psychology what chemistry did for alchemy, challenging dominant scripts. At the least, neuroscience will compliment, interrogate, dislodge, or echo existing critical modes; the affective disorders will serve as sites of inquiry into language and the composing brain.

What happens, neurologically, when writers write, and what happens when writing breaks down? My purpose is twofold:

1. To encourage new research into affective illness in composition studies. First of all, by "neuroscience", I do not mean the explication of poems via fMRI, or the reduction of art to neat pathological categories. Empiricism and positivism are not synonymous. Jack and Applebaum, in "This Is Your Brain on Rhetoric", suggest a new "neurorhetorics": an examination of the neuroscience of rhetoric and the rhetoric of neuroscience.
2. To explore critical spaces beyond the psychiatry versus anti-psychiatry debate. We study all manner of difference: race, gender, class. Why not affective difference?

Manic–depressive illness is among the most painful of human maladies, capable of producing anguish beyond anguish. Affective illness was described by Hippocrates, demonized in the Middle Ages, idealized in the Renaissance, and medicalized since the Enlightenment (Solomon 295). Since antiquity, those who live with affective disorders have been alternately demonized and romanticized. In *The Republic,* Plato claimed that "no mad or senseless person can be a friend of God" (Book II). Yet in *Phaedrus,* his Socrates upholds the necessity of divinely inspired madness:

> Madness comes from God, whereas sober sense is merely human.... If a man comes to the door of poetry untouched by madness, believing that technique alone will make him a good poet, he and his sane companions never reach perfection, but are eclipsed by the performances of the madman.

Unfortunately, Socrates does not reveal how to differentiate between "inspired" madness and "merely human" mental illness. In general, the Platonic tradition upholds *sōphrosýnē*, or healthy-mindedness – the neat logic of Aristotle's golden mean. But madness tends to unravel neat packages. When manic, Virginia Woolf could talk for three days straight, whether or not in the presence of an audience; her action was not appetitive, a violation of moderation. Woolf suffered from a mental illness. The Platonic concept of appetite-as-archenemy would be used for two millennia to blame the mentally ill for their suffering.

For Kimberly Emmons, depression itself is a rhetorical phenomenon, a "dynamic entity at the intersection of physical, cognitive and emotional realities" (1). As such, it is "particularly vulnerable to the means of its own articulation" (1). For Emmons, the affective disorders are ideal for rhetorical analysis; because they lack a physiological diagnostic test, the disorders "become visible, or remain invisible, through the language used to describe them" (1). Emmons applies Susan Sontag's theory to observe that mental illness, like tuberculosis, is ascribed to irrational, personality-based theories, often on the part of the "rational".

In my own times of depressive madness, the mute void of writer's block – a black wordlessness – descends quietly, like a mantle of lead. In this state, I could more easily climb K2 than generate an essay. Fragments of ideas, a word here or there, a disconnected sentence – I ruminate on each endlessly, erasing Penelope-like every word I manage to commit. These erasures are a matter of survival; the world is a hostile audience, and each word carries potential for vast ridicule.

As far as I know, no one has ever ridiculed my work. But there is always a first time.

Writer's block: derailed, disengaged, disembodied

> I sit down religiously every morning. In the course of a working day of eight hours, I write three sentences, which I erase before leaving the table in despair.
>
> Joseph Conrad

> A great ox stands on my tongue.
>
> Aeschylus

Psychoanalyst Edmond Bergler coined "writer's block" in the 1950s with "The Writer and Psychoanalysis", in which he called "creative" writing "an expression of unconscious defenses against masochistic conflicts; writer's block [is] the result of the breakdown of these defenses" (Rose 13). Bergler questioned the efficacy of then-current phallic and anal phase analysis in working with "inhibited writers" (13). Since Bergler, however, writer's block has been largely excluded from the mainstream of critical discourse, a "shadowy pseudo-phenomenon" (Kantor 4). Keith Hjortshoj finds remarkable "the peculiar silence surrounding a malady that has such devastating effects on the lives of serious, capable writers" (9).

For blocked writers, the writing process is infused with anxiety, frustration, shame, and/or anger. Secrecy, missed deadlines, and binge writing are common. Some compose excruciatingly slowly, or produce only "false starts, repetitions, blind alleys, or disconnected fragments of discourse" (Rose 3). Severely affected writers speak the language of depression; they are "immobilized, motionless, stranded, mired, derailed, disengaged, disembodied, paralyzed and numb" (Hjortshoj 9). Despite the pathos of these descriptors, cognitivists like Rose and Zachary Leader view the phenomenon as mainly cognitive in etiology, the result of premature sentence-level editing, in which writers stymie themselves with rigid rules like "Never end a sentence with a preposition." In this view, any affective turbulence is the effect of the writer's difficulties with writing – not the cause.

To use the cognitivists' definition, "writer's block" occurs "when a writer is unable to write when writing is wanted, and the writer has something to say", or is "unable to begin writing, or continue writing, for reasons other than a lack of basic skill or commitment" (Rose 3). Martin Kantor, author of the psychiatric manual on writer's block, calls block "a severe and global composing process dysfunction" often linked to depression and manic–depressive illness (2). Writer's block is not procrastination, although blocked writers almost always commit this painful form of self-abuse. Nor are blocks "writing delays" – when writers stop just to think, strategize, or negotiate the slipperiness of language. The classic manifestations of writer's block mimic those of depression, including escalating self-criticism and decreased enjoyment of the writing task (Kantor 117). For me, memory – not to mention working memory – simply goes away. The chorus weighs in, with its notes of fear *(This time, they'll see that I don't know what I'm doing)* and shame *(Narcissist!)*. In the silence of the blank page, the blocked writer finds a twisted form of solace; for Mallarmé, *le vide papier, que sa blancheur defend.*

Neuroscience promises exploration into what happens when we write, and when writing breaks down. In a 2005 study, Alice Flaherty examined frontal and temporal lobe changes that "may result in decreased idea generation" – perhaps the "sparse speech and cognitive inflexibility" of depression (what Kantor called its "miasmic silence"), a state that "drains away meaning" (121). In a 2010 study, Johns Hopkins researcher Alan Braun, a jazz musician, observed musical composition and improvisation using fMRI technology. Braun's study suggests that the metabolic processes of the dorsolateral prefrontal cortex, an area of the front of the brain, actually slowed down during improvisation: "This area is linked to self-censoring, such as carefully deciding what words you might say on a job interview. Shutting down this area could lower inhibitions.... When you're telling your own musical story, you're shutting down impulses that might impede the flow of novel ideas."

Some writers are more adept at this than others. In Kantor's clinical experience, writing blocks "are unknown in the grandiose, the artist who truly believes that everyone is waiting for them to produce, who has the attitude of 'If they don't like what I do, that's too bad – not for me, but for them!'" (26). This enviable attitude is not available to all. Kantor describes one depressed academic who:

> hesitated to write and publish because she felt both she and her works were not up to standard. Her "little voices" told her "You don't have what it takes to make it in the big city," [and] "That's too quirky to be appealing." Consequently, she wrote bland, washed-out impersonal works to avoid revealing herself.... Her tight, desiccated works displeased her critics, who condemned her writing as "cold," full of what one critic termed "unemotional outbursts." (83)

This writer is a long way from "Never end a sentence with a preposition."

To their credit, Rose and Leader are among the very few writers on this subject in 30 years of composition studies. A cognitivist theory, however, largely excludes "psychological problems" – an action profound in its dismissiveness, its New Critical horror of the personal, the closing off worlds of experience. In this view, the writer's task is simply to "replace dysfunctional rules with functional rules" (Rose 16). Yet the agony of Conrad's – and my – blocked writing (three lines in eight hours, then erase) suggests something deeper. Melville, Woolf, Hemingway, Ralph Ellison, and David Foster Wallace knew the torments of block. Dickens, in a pique while composing *Little Dorrit*, found himself:

> Prowling about the rooms, sitting down, getting up, stirring the fire, looking out of [the] window, tearing my hair, sitting down to write, writing nothing, writing something and tearing it up, going out, coming in, a Monster to my family, a dread Phenomenon to myself. ("Letter" 1856)

The blocked Henry James' vicious volleys of self-contempt also seem to be drawn from deep emotional wells: "I have [an] unspeakable reaction against my smallness of production; my wretched habits of work, or unwork... my perpetual failure to focus my attention, to look things in the face, to invent, to produce, in a word" (45).

Alice Brand has asserted that "no cognitive model, even a social/cognitive model, is adequate" to describe writing, an infinitely complex orchestration of language, cognition, emotion, and memory. This is not to say the cognitivist approach should be replaced by an emotivist one; rather, a blended approach is needed. In neuroscience, *emotions* are defined as "organized brain responses to events in the outer world; [they] are absolutely critical to decision-making" (Wang). The writer's brain is the sky where near-infinite events collide; the ensuing weather systems warrant meteorological research.

On writing and mania

> Flowers are restful to look at. They have neither emotions nor conflicts.
> Freud
>
> Little poppies, little hell flames/Do you do no harm?/It exhausts me to watch you.
> Sylvia Plath, "Poppies in July" (203, ll. 1–2)

For those of us who live with manic–depressive illness, mania turns up the gain, intensifying perception – particularly of color and light. Van Gogh called mania "a terrible lucidity"; Robert Lowell deemed it "a magical orange grove in a nightmare". Today, PET and SPECT scans of manic brain metabolism glow like storms (in scan color schemas, manic brains literally glow brighter than depressed brains; storms of red, orange, and yellow contrast to depression's blues and greens). Andreasen, in a second study at Iowa, compared non-affected writers to non-writers hospitalized for hypomania, suggesting "The neurological state of hypomania [mild mania] mimics the state of creative activity in non-affected writers" (Andreasen and Powers 282). Yet depression and mania are not the roots of poetry; it would be overreaching to make such a claim. Among Andreasen's manic non-writers, writing "is facilitated because of the rapid flow of ideas in mania, and the falling of inhibitions; yet [art] is produced only in very mild cases and when the patient is otherwise talented" (Goodwin and Jamison 33). The following poem, "God Is an Herbivore", was written "without pause, in a few minutes" by a hypomanic non-poet in a psychiatric facility (Goodwin and Jamison 26). Kay Jamison sees in the poem "the infectious cadence, tangential and loose language, frequent punning, fast, flowing rhythm, and recurrent sexual references" characteristic of hypomania:

> Thyme passes, mixed with long grasses of the field.
> Rosemary weeps into meadow sweeps.
> While curry is favored by the sun in its heaven...
> Hash is itself: high by being.
> Laws say shallots shall not – so they shant.
> But the coriander meanders, the cumin seeds come.... (26)

The neurochemical cascade of mania can result in accelerated, pressured cognition (*DSM-V*). John Ruskin described the "flood of ideas" of manic euphoria: "I am giddy with the quantity of things in my head – trains of thought beginning and branching to infinity, crossing each other, and all tempting and wanting to be worked out" (xiv).

Such perception, such extremes of mood, cannot help but color invention. Plath's colors, her painterly vision – *ut pictura poesis* – was, for Adam Kirsch, "so heightened that the ordinary becomes strange"; of course, this is a definition of poetry itself (241). Emily Dickinson's nature poems spoke with this shimmering, almost vibratory intensity; Van Gogh saw wheeling, painfully intense stars (Kirsch 153).

In mania and hypomania, energies ascend, and inhibitions drop. Early studies, like those of Emil Kraepelin, suggested that rhymes, punning, sound association, and original responses to word association tasks increase during mania; newer studies also suggest enhanced rhyming ability and "expressional fluency" – "the creative juxtaposition of words, phrases and sentences" (Andreasen and Powers 72). Patients in an affective disorders clinic performed more fluently than controls on word association tasks (Pons et al.). Mania also brings "combinatory thinking", wherein ideas become rapid and flexible, "extravagantly combined and elaborated" (Andreasen and Powers 397). One friend described Woolf's manic spinning of tales as "dazzling performances", "wild generalizations...embroidered with elaborate fantasy, sent up like rockets...one would hand her a bit of information as dull as a lump of lead, [and] she would hand it back glittering like diamonds" (Caramagno 49). Alice Flaherty, a writer and neurologist, writes of her own experience with hypergraphia, a rare manic compulsion to write day and night, even taking a grease pencil into the shower (30).

Robert Lowell responded to lithium, which ended his hospitalizations and enabled him to write. Not all bipolar writers are so fortunate. Some claim medication blunts invention; this alone carries rich potential for composition studies. In a 1986 study in *The American Journal of Psychiatry*, researchers discontinued lithium in 22 people taking the drug for bipolar disorder, and the participants showed an increase in associational productivity and verbal fluency (Shaw et al. 1986). Restoring the lithium "significantly reversed" these effects (1166). Some writers are simply unwilling to give up the highs; to complicate a writer's dilemma, a "creativity mystique" exists, in which artists are urged to refuse medication for the sake of art (Pryal 5). Peter Kramer writes on "heroic melancholy", in which depression's "tortures somehow ennoble, and are the source of creativity" (37).

Whether or not Whitman had the manic–depressive gene, he captured its moments of what the Greeks called *ekstasis,* a Charlie Sheenian invincibility: "O the joy of my spirit – it is uncaged – it darts like lightning! It is not enough to have this globe or a certain time/I will have thousands of globes, and all the time!" ("Poem of Joys" 192). One student contrasted her writing during manic and depressed states: "When I'm hypomanic, I can write a paper in two hours – you know, proving the existence of God using string theory. But I can't proofread it. That would mean sitting still for two extra minutes. Now when I'm depressed, I proofread very well – but it takes me six hours" ("Julie").

In a metastudy of manic–depressive illness across professions, "more poets than any other group regarded intense moods as integral and necessary to what they did and how they did it" (Goodwin and Jamison 335). Half of bipolar writers reported euphoric states prior to intense bursts of creative activity. For a third, however, dysphoria also heralds the creative burst (392).

Sylvia Plath and a poetics of madness

> Madness is terrific I can assure you, and not to be sniffed at; in its lava I still find most of the things I write about. It shoots out of one everything shaped, final, not in mere driblets, as sanity does.
>
> Virginia Woolf (Zwerding 254)

The year 2013 marks the fiftieth anniversary of Sylvia Plath's suicide. The Plath critical bookshelf strains under half a century of biographically informed readings, many of which declaim biographical criticism. For some, the *Ariel* poems (Plath's last) are indictments of the multitudinous shortcomings of Ted Hughes, "Daddy" Plath, and others. Plath inspires aversion; some critics have named her an "Oedipal victim", a "bitch-goddess", a "monster who, in the end, choked on her hatred of humanity." I prefer the view of Joyce Carol Oates: "[Plath] is less dramatic than all of this, and therefore more valuable."

In "Mourning and Melancholia", Freud posited that the melancholic has "a keener eye for the truth than other people who are not melancholic" (246). Depression renders one painfully attuned to emotional sky and wind, to approaching storms. Plath's many biographers – whether or not they use the term "manic–depression" (most do not), have long commented on the poet's sparkling creative highs, her rages, and her savage, debilitating depressions. Seldom do critics contemplate the mental illness that took her life, or how its cycles of ecstasy and despair inform her art; indeed, many go to comic lengths to avoid engaging with mental illness. (One critic I read described Plath, who died with her head in an oven, "a supposedly suicidal poet".)

How might mania inform readings of *Ariel*? Delusions of grandiosity often occur in this state. During his "pathological enthusiasms", Lowell believed he could stop traffic with his stare; Plath's journal expresses "frustration" that her powers fall short of godlike. She would be "the Poetess of America", the apotheosis of a tradition extending from Sappho through Elizabeth Browning, Christina Rossetti, Emily Dickinson, and Marianne Moore. On 28 August 1957, she wrote, excitedly, that "the work of Adrienne Cecile Rich will soon be eclipsed by these eight poems. I am eager, chafing, sure of my gift" (360). Is this grandiosity? Or a keener vision?

Severe depression manifests a phenomenon called "early-morning awakening", a sleep-phase disturbance characterized by nightmare visions of violence, pain, and death. Milton's *L'Allegro* speaks of "horrid shapes, and shrieks, and sights unholy". In *Giving Up: The Last Days of Sylvia Plath*, Plath's friend Jillian Becker reports the poet's final nights, when, "I heard her calling me, and she'd say, 'This is the worst time, this hour of morning'" (12). *Ariel* is replete with images from this early-morning realm of nightmare. The female body of "The Jailer" is not only raped, but "hung, starved, burned, and hooked" (226, line 35).

In "Totem": "In the bowl the hare is aborted, Its baby head out of the way... /Flayed of fur and humanity" (264, ll. 11–13). The taproot of Plath's ruminative depression inches ever deeper, into dark aquifers of human evil and suffering, of Dachau, Auschwitz, severed-foot paperweights. From "Three Women": "I am accused./I dream of massacres./I am garden of black and red agonies./I drink them,/Hating myself, hating and fearing" (180, stanza 22).

The label "confessional", branded on Plath's generation of American poets, is reductive. For Oates, *Ariel* is "not one woman dragging her shadow around in a circle". The poems are not emotional outbursts. Rather, personae exist in the realm of the uncanny, in "the light of the mind/cold and planetary" (172, line 1). In *Ariel*, we witness a self approaching the event horizon of a black hole – "and the universe slides from my side" (208, l. 62). We witness the spaghettification of a self, torn atom from atom by some inconceivable gravity. The poems are sometimes horrific in their implications. "Edge" carries a quiet suggestion of Medea, of child killing:

> The woman is perfected.
> Her dead body wears the smile of accomplishment...
> Each dead child is coiled, a white serpent
> One at each little Pitcher of milk, now empty.
> She has folded them back into her body as petals
> Of a rose close when the garden
> Stiffens and odors bleed.... (273, ll. 1–16)

In the "black amnesias of heaven" (250, line 21), no one attends but the moon, and "The moon has nothing to be sad about/Staring down from her hood of bone./She is used to this sort of thing./Her blacks crackle and drag" (273, ll. 18–21). "These poems stun me", said Anne Sexton, Plath's friend and fellow death junkie. "They eat time."

In "Elm", Plath's embodied tree is "scathed" by soft moonlight. Despite its "great taproot", it neither enjoys nor produces greenness or shade. Rather, it suffers the "atrocity of sunsets/scorched to the root" (192, ll. 16–18). "I know the bottom", says the tree. "And it is what you fear" (192, ll. 1–2). It even speaks of some felt tree pathology: "I am terrified by this dark thing that sleeps in me./All day I feel its soft, feathery turnings, its malignity" (192, ll. 31–33).

In "Tulips", the dysphoric speaker turns from too-vivid color and toward the elemental whiteness of her hospital room. The tulips suggest mania's heightened perception of color and light; shimmering and rustling, they violate the speaker's white sanctum. The damn things just won't go away: "The tulips are too red in the first place, they hurt me.../ Their redness talks to my wound, it corresponds" (161 ll. 36 and 49).

The title poem, "Ariel", is less a "white Godiva" galloping through pre-dawn darkness (surely, a Freudian field event) than a suicide poem. Its destination – "the cauldron of morning" – recalls the nightmarish phenomenon of early-morning awakening. The mount, "Ariel", is an arc of brown neck in darkness. Then, "something" – an unnamed force – unseats the rider, hurling her into space, "Thighs, hair, flakes from my heels": "I unpeel/Dead hands, dead stringencies" (239 ll. 12–13, 16). The isolation of madness is complete: "I am the arrow/The dew that flies/ Suicidal, at one with the drive/Into the red/Eye, the cauldron of morning" (239 ll. 27–28, 30).

Many read the poem "Ariel" as a will-to-power, with suicide a purposeful and empowering choice, an artist's chosen escape from the stultifying culture of the early 1960s. But an alternate reading, with affective disorder in mind, is that of a body/mind hurtling out of control. An arrow, a powerful image for psychoanalytic criticism, also implies powerlessness; once fired, an arrow cannot change its course. "Something else" lifts this rider, bodily. "Dead hands, dead stringencies", dead efforts to hold things together, all of these "unpeel" for good; the speaker will not survive the "cauldron of morning".

Plath's art navigates both dark undercurrents and icy altitudes; the poems offer a front-row seat to the terrifying instability of the self. Plath wrote through manic–depression, swimming against its tide as long as she could before eventually succumbing. Suicide is less rational choice than the unpeeling from life – gradual or sudden – of a psyche in extremis. Plath provides a richer source than mere "Oedipal victim", "bitch–goddess", or "monster choking on her hatred of humanity". "Ariel" may well be her apologia of the act of suicide, for an audience she knew well would await.

Works cited

American College Health Association. *National College Health Assessment II: Reference Group Report 2012*. Web. 14 December 2012.
American Psychiatric Association. *DSM-V: The Diagnostic and Statistical Manual of Mental Disorders*. dsm5.org. 27 May 2013. Web. 10 June 2013.

Andreasen, Nancy J. C. "Creativity and Mental Illness: Prevalence Rates in Writers and First-Degree Relatives". *American Journal of Psychiatry*, 1987. 144(10): 1288–1292. *PubMed.gov*. US National Library of Medicine. Web. 1 June 2012.

——. and Ira Glick. "Bipolar Affective Disorder and Creativity: Implications and Clinical Management". *Comprehensive Psychiatry*, 1988. 29(3): 207–317. *PubMed.gov*. US National Library of Medicine. Web. 24 February 2013.

——. and Pauline S. Powers. "Creativity and Psychosis: An Examination of Conceptual Style". *Archives of General Psychiatry*, 1975. 32(1): 70–73. *PubMed.gov*. US National Library of Medicine. Web. 01 June 2012.

Aristotle. "Problemata". *The Works of Aristotle Translated into English*. Vol. VII. Oxford: Clarendon Press, 1971. Print.

Brand, Alice. "Writing, Emotion and the Brain: What Graduate School Taught Me About Healing". Keynote Address, Assembly for Expanded Perspectives on Learning. The Conference on College Composition and Communication, Atlanta, GA. 24 March 1994.

Becker, Jillian. *Giving Up: The Last Days of Sylvia Plath*. New York: St. Martin's, 2002. Print.

Bergler, Edmund, M.D. "Unconscious Mechanisms in Writer's Block". *The Psychoanalytic Review*, 1955. 42: 160–167. Print.

Byron. *The Works of Lord Byron, Volume V*. Philadelphia: Henry Carey Baird, 1853. GoogleBooks. Web. 2 February 2013.

The Centers for Disease Control. "Current Depression among Adults, United States". *Cdc.gov*. Web. 2 June 2013.

Caramagno, Thomas C. *The Flight of the Mind: Virginia Woolf's Art and Manic-Depressive Illness*. Berkeley: California UP, 1992. Print.

Dickens, Charles. "'A Monster to My Family': A Letter from Charles Dickens to Miss Burdett-Coutts, 19 February 1856". *The Morgan Library and Museum Blog*. The Morgan Library. 20 December 2011. Web. 3 February 2013.

Emmons, Kimberly. *Black Dogs and Blue Words: Depression and Gender in the Age of Self-Care*. New Brunswick, NJ: Rutgers UP, 2010. Print.

Flaherty, Alice. *The Midnight Disease: The Drive to Write, Writer's Block, and the Creative Brain*. New York: Mariner Books, 2004. Print.

Forgeard, Marie. "Linguistic Styles of Eminent Writers Suffering from Unipolar and Bipolar Mood Disorder". *Creativity Research Journal*. Philadelphia: 2008. 20(1 81). *Tandfonline.com*. Taylor and Francis. Web. 16 November 2012.

DOI: 10.1057/9781137381668

Foucault, Michel. *Madness and Civilization: A History of Insanity in the Age of Reason*. New York: Random House, 1965. Print.
Freud, Sigmund. "Mourning and Melancholia". Trans. James Strachey and Anna Freud. *The Standard Edition of the Complete Psychological Works of Sigmund Freud, Vol. XIV*. London: Hogarth Press, 1917. *GoogleBooks*. Web. 1 February 2013.
Frost, Robert. "To be a poet [...]". *brainyquote.com*. BookRags Media Network, 2013. Web. 12 June 2013.
Galvez, et al. "Positive Aspects of Mental Illness: A Review in Bipolar Disorder". *Journal of Affective Disorders*, February 2011. 128(3): 185–190. *PubMed.gov*. US National Library of Medicine. Web. 2 February 2013.
Greaves, Robert. Qtd. in Kaufman, J. C., and Sexton, J. D. "Why Doesn't the Writing Cure Help Poets?" *Review of General Psychology*, 2006. 10(3): 268–282. doi:10.1037/1089-2680.10.3.268
Goodwin, Frederick, and Kay Redfield Jamison. *Manic–Depressive Illness*. 1st ed. New York: Oxford UP, 1990. Print.
——. *Manic–Depressive Illness: Bipolar Disorders and Recurrent Depression*. 2nd ed. Oxford: Oxford UP, 2007. 397–407. Print.
"Julie". Student interview. Georgia State University, 2 March 2010.
Jack, Jordynn, and L.G. Applebaum. " 'This Is Your Brain on Rhetoric': Research Directions for Neurorhetorics". *Rhetoric Society Quarterly*, 2010. 40(5): 411–437. *tandfonline*. Taylor & Francis. Web. 15 April 2012.
James, Henry. *The Notebooks of Henry James*. Ed. Matthiessen, F.O. and Kenneth Murdock. Oxford: Oxford UP, 1947. Print. 12 February 2012.
Jamison, Kay Redfield. *Touched with Fire: Manic–Depressive Illness and the Artistic Imagination*. New York: Simon Schuster, 1993. Print.
Hjortshoj, Keith. *Understanding Writing Blocks*. Oxford: Oxford UP, 2001. Print.
Kantor, Martin. "Affective Spectrum Disorder Block". In Kantor, Martin. *Understanding Writer's Block: A Therapist's Guide to Diagnosis and Treatment*. Westport, CT: Praeger, 1995. 27–45. Print.
Kaufman, James. "Genius, Lunatics, And Poets: Mental Illness In Prize-Winning Authors". *Imagination, Cognition and Personality*, 2000-1. 20(4): 305–314. *Baywood.metapress.com*. Web. 20 June 2013.
——. "The Sylvia Plath Effect: Mental Illness in Eminent Creative Writers". *Journal of Creative Behavior*, 2001. 35(1): 37–50. *Onlinelibrary.wiley.com*. Wiley Online Library. Web. 11 June 2013.

Kirsch, Adam. *The Wounded Surgeon: Confession and Transformation in Six American Poets: Lowell, Bishop, Berryman, Jarrell, Schwartz, and Plath*. New York: Norton, 2004. Print.
Kramer, Peter. *Against Depression*. New York: Penguin, 2005.
Kristeva, Julia. *Black Sun: Depression and Melancholia*. New York: Columbia UP, 1989. Print.
Lehrer, Jonah. "Depression's Upside". *nytimes.com*. *The New York Times*. 25 February 2010. Web. 28 January 2011.
Leader, Zachary. *Writer's Block*. Baltimore: Johns Hopkins UP, 1991. Print.
Limb, C.J., and Alan Braun. "'This Is Your Brain on Jazz': Researchers Use fMRI to Study Improvisation". *hopkinsmedical.org*. Johns Hopkins Medical Institutions. 26 February 2008. Web. 1 February 2013.
Lowell, Robert. "Robert Lowell". *Poetrymountain.com*. Ed. John Struloeff. Poetry Mountain: An Online Poetry Archive. Web. 4 February 2013.
Ludwig, Arnold. "Creative Achievement and Psychopathology: Comparison among Professions". *American Journal of Psychotherapy*, 1992. 46(3): 330–356. Web. *Europepmc.org*. Europe PubMed Central. Web. 10 June 2013.
Mallarmé, Stephané. Qtd. in Presto, Jenifer. "Unbearable Burdens: Aleksandr Blok and the Modernist Resistance to Progeny and Domesticity". *Slavic Review*, 2004. 63(1): 6.
Martin, Emily. *Bipolar Expeditions: Mania and Depression in American Culture*. Princeton, NJ: Princeton UP, 2007. Print.
Micciche, Laura. *Doing Emotion: Rhetoric, Writing, Teaching*. Portsmouth, NH: Boynton/Cook, 2007. Print.
Milton, John. *L'Allegro. The Complete Poetry and Essential Prose of John Milton*. Ed. William Kerrigan. New York: Modern Library, 2007.
Moffitt, Kathie, et al. "Depression and Memory Narrative Type". *Journal of Abnormal Psychology*, 1994. 103(3): 581–583. *PsychNet.apa.org*. The American Psychological Association. Web. 12 March 2013.
Murrough, James, et al. "Cognitive Dysfunction in Depression: Neurocircuitry and New Therapeutic Strategies". *Neurobiology of Learning and Memory*, 2011. 96(4): 553–563. *PubMed.gov*. US National Library of Medicine. Web. 21 January 2013.
Nietzsche, Friedrich. *Thus Spake Zarathustra*. Google e-book. Algora Publishing, 2003. 29.
Oates, Joyce Carol. "The Death Throes of Romanticism: The Poetry of Sylvia Plath". In *The Southern Review*, 1973. *Docstoc.com*. N.p. Web. 12 June 2012.

Plato. *Phaedrus*. Trans. Benjamin Jowett. *The Internet Classics Archive*. Web. 20 June 2013.

——. *The Republic*. Trans. Benjamin Jowett. *The Internet Classics Archive*. Web. 20 June 2013.

Plath, Sylvia. "A Birthday Present," "Ariel," "Edge," "Elm," "The Jailer," "Poppies in July," "The Moon and the Yew Tree," "Three Women," "Totem," "Tulips." In *Sylvia Plath: The Collected Poems*. New York: Harper Perennial, 1992. Print.

——. *The Unabridged Journals of Sylvia Plath, 1950–1962*. New York: Anchor Books. Ed. Karen V. Kukil, 2009. Print.

Pons, L., et al. "Mood-Independent Aberrancies in Associative Processes in Bipolar Affective Disorder: An Apparent Stabilizing Effect of Lithium". *Psychiatry Research*, 1985. 14(4): 315–322. *PubMed.gov*. US National Library of Medicine. Web. 2 July 2012.

Pryal, Katie Rose Guest. "The Creativity Mystique and the Rhetoric of Mood Disorders". *Disability Studies Quarterly*, 2011. 31(3). *Academia.edu*. "Katie Rose Guest Pryal". 1 January 2011. Web. 2 February 2013.

Rose, Mike, Ed. *When a Writer Can't Write: Studies in Writer's Block and Other Composing-Process Problems*. New York: Guilford, 1985. Print.

Ruskin, John. *The Complete Works of John Ruskin, Vol. 19*. Ed. Edward Cook and Alexander Wedderburn. London: George Allen, 1905. *GoogleBooks*. Web. 22 August 2011.

Shaw, E.D., et al. "Effects of Lithium Carbonate on Associative Productivity and Idiosyncrasy in Bipolar Outpatients". *American Journal of Psychiatry*, 1986. 143: 1166–1169. *PubMed.gov*. US National Library of Medicine. Web. 1 February 2013.

Solomon, Andrew. *The Noonday Demon: An Atlas of Depression*. New York: Simon and Schuster, 2001. Print.

Stirman, A. and James Pennebaker. "Word Use in the Poetry of Suicidal and Non-Suicidal Poets". *Psychosomatic Medicine*, 2001. 63(4): 517–522. *PubMed.gov*. US National Library of Medicine. Web. 4 July 2010.

Styron, William. *Darkness Visible: A Memoir of Madness*. New York: Vintage, 1992.

Thomas, Katherine, et al. "Depressed Writing: Cognitive Distortions in the Works of Depressed and Non-Depressed Poets and Writers". *Psychology of Aesthetics, Creativity and the Arts*, November 2007. 1(4): 204–218. *PsychNet.apa.org*. The American Psychological Association. Web. 20 February 2013.

Turnera, Arlene, et al. "Association Between Subcortical Volumes and Verbal Memory in Unmedicated Depressed Patients and Healthy Controls". *Neuropsychologia*, July 2012. 50(9): 2348–2355. *PsychNet.apa. org*. The American Psychological Association. Web. 20 November 2012.

Vatz, Richard. "Psychiatry". In *Encyclopedia of Rhetoric and Composition: Communication from Ancient Times to the Information Age*. Ed. Theresa Enos. New York: Taylor and Francis, 1996. Print.

Wang, Sam. *The Neuroscience of Everyday Life*. Chantilly, VA: The Teaching Company, 2010.

Watts, Fraser, and Zafra Cooper. "The Effects of Depression on Structural Aspects of the Recall of Prose". *Journal of Abnormal Psychology*, May 1989. 98(2): 150–153. *PubMed.gov*. The US National Library of Medicine. Web. 2 January 2012.

Whitman, Walt. "Poem of Joys". *The Poems of Walt Whitman/Leaves of Grass*. New York: Thomas Y. Crowell Co., 1902. *GoogleBooks*. Web. 12 January 2013.

World Health Organization. "Media Centre: Depression Fact Sheet". October 2012. *Who.org*. World Health Organization. Web. 12 October 2012.

Zwerding, Alex. *Virginia Woolf and the Real World*. Berkeley: California UP, 1986.

2
Muse Afire: Negotiating the Line between Creative Pursuit and Mental Illness

Nancer Ballard

Abstract: *Ballard's essay deftly explores links between art and affective disorder through artists like Tchaikovsky, for whom "[A] sense of bliss... comes over me [when] a new idea awakens in me... I forget everything and behave like a mad man. Everything within me starts pulsing and quivering....". Tracing personifications of "the muse" since Hesiod's* Theogony, *Ballard is struck by a friend's casual question over lunch: "If you were assured of writing something enduring, would you agree to be mentally ill?" Those who devote themselves to art face the same void that people with affective illness face every day, Ballard writes – a void from which something may be made from nothing – a heightening of emotional and perceptual intensity, linguistic acuity, existential preoccupation, and deepening levels of awareness.*

Keywords: Art and the affective disorders; the muse; emotional intensity; affective illness; levels of awareness

Horton, Stephanie Stone, ed. *Affective Disorder and the Writing Life: The Melancholic Muse.* Basingstoke: Palgrave Macmillan, 2014. DOI: 10.1057/9781137381668.

> When thou shalt have allotted me my fire, I will not fare here from the dark again.
>
> Homer, *The Iliad*

After attending a lecture on the role of depression in Virginia Woolf's novels, a friend and I sat in the Boston Public Library café naming other writers stalked by psychiatric illnesses – Sylvia Plath, Hermann Hesse, William Blake.... Once we branched out to composers and painters, the list became too long to hold our attention – Vincent Van Gogh, Kurt Cobain, Edvard Munch, Peter Tchaikovsky.... "What about you?" my friend asked. "If you were assured of writing something enduring, would you agree to be mentally ill?" I glance away, waiting for the sudden clench in my throat to clear. We pay our bill and say goodnight, but on the way home I wonder why there's such a strong link between creativity and mental illness. No one asks athletes if they would be willing to be mentally ill. Are artists drawn to craziness? Does insanity creep toward them?

Darkness and a thousand cartwheels

In *The Noonday Demon: An Atlas of Depression*, Alexander Solomon describes our notions of depression as having gone through a thousand cartwheels since it was first studied in ancient Greece. Mental illness, an even broader category, is notoriously difficult to pin down: our minds are mutable; our brains are integrated with our bodies in complex ways; we are in constant dynamic relationship with a changing environment, and much of what affects and compels us goes on below consciousness. We also can't see the "mind", so mental and emotional illnesses have to be defined circumstantially.

In the bible of psychological diagnosis, the *Diagnostic and Statistical Manual of Mental Disorders,* mental illness is defined as thinking, expressions of feeling, or behavior that disturbs a person's ability to function in his or her culture, or causes the person significant continuing distress. This definition covers a lot of ground, especially as mental illness symptoms wax and wane, and some very distressed people are highly functional whereas some barely functional people are not distressed. Mental illness can be the black cloud that darkens your vision or blankness where once there were thoughts. It can be visions before you, or voices outside you, or images you know aren't real but can't shake. It can be a belief that you are directed by God, or a conviction that you are worthless and what you do does not count. Illness can flood you with sensations, or leave you so empty you feel you hardly exist. Mental illness is experiencing extremes of what non-mentally ill people experience in everyday life and not knowing what's coming next.

Coaxing something from nothing

Who willingly plunges into that unknown? Those propelled by the unconscious, which is, by definition, unknown. Those already lost looking for home, glory, or a way out of darkness. Those drawn to possibility or risk. And those who awaken in an unknown land and need to make sense of their surroundings or predicaments. Artists and writers must clamber into the unknown, as they are searching for something that doesn't already exist. In *The Creative Habit: Learn It and Use It For Life*, Choreographer Twyla Tharp describes walking into her empty studio 5 weeks before she is scheduled to present 8 performances in front of 1,200 people:

> In five weeks I'm flying to Los Angeles with a troupe of six dancers...I have half the program in hand – a fifty-minute ballet for all six dancers set to Beethoven's twenty-ninth piano sonata.... I created the piece more than a year ago...and I've spent the past few weeks rehearsing it with the company.
>
> The other half of the program is a mystery. I don't know what music I'll be using. I don't know which dancers I'll be working with. I have no idea what the costumes will look like, or the lighting, or who will be performing the music. I have no idea of the piece, although it has to be long enough to fill the second half of a full program to give the paying audience its money's worth.

When Tharp observes, "To some people this empty room symbolizes something profound, mysterious, and terrifying", I know I'd be right in that camp, but what follows next takes my breath away, for it's the pursuit I know well – "the task of starting with nothing and working your way toward creating something whole and beautiful and satisfying". Whether staring at a blank computer screen, scowling at white canvas, or sitting at the piano with hands hovering over the keys, those who devote themselves to art face the same void that many people with mental illness face every day.

From muse to mind

The ancients tell us that nothing exists, not even gods, when there is no one to tell. In Mesopotamia and ancient Greece, muses were believed to help humans create songs and stories to serve and preserve themselves, their world, and the gods. The word "muse" is likely derived from the Indo-European root "*mem*", meaning "to think". It is also the source of the Greek word "*Mnemosyne*" or "memory" and the goddess of Memory. The English words "mental", "mentor", and "demented" share this same root.

Most of us picture the Muses as the nine daughters of Zeus and the goddess of Memory, but older Greek stories tell of three Muses: one born from the movement of water, another who makes sound by striking the air, and a third who is embodied only in the human voice. On my next visit to the Boston Public Library, I notice two larger-than-life muses sitting outside on the steps. The one on the left is cloaked in a drape that covers her head and encircles her shoulders. In her outstretched hand, resting on the arm of the bench on which she sits, she holds a palm-sized sphere. A fortune teller's gazing ball? The celestial globe of an astronomer? She regards it calmly, expectantly, with a trace of concern. From the bottom of the steps, beneath her gaze, she seems kind, gentle, like a serene nun in a habit. From the front, her hooded eyes and heavy lids make her look as if she's been crying.

The things that aren't there

According to my high school humanities class, the litmus test for mental illness was perceptual disturbances. Do you hear voices? Do you see things that aren't there? Of course, I wanted to say. How could we think if we didn't hear voices in our heads or imagine things? When I finally did ask – my mother, as I recall – she told me that this wasn't what people meant. "Everyone does that, it's only when you believe they are real that it's dangerous."

According to the American Psychiatric Association, hallucinations and delusions not only harass those with delusional disorders and schizophrenia, but can also show up during major depressive episodes and mania. The line between vivifying images that an audience will respond to as if they are real and being possessed by images that have taken on a life of their own can be a fine one. Painter and psychoanalyst

DOI: 10.1057/9781137381668

Marion Milner discovered that line when she tried to recreate the color she'd seen at the edge of a field on a summer holiday:

> I recalled the colour of the grass-edge between stubble field and sea-shore, the mixed pale green and creamy yellow of sun bleached August grass; and as I watched the memory of the colour it seemed to change and grow in vividness. This feeling of colour as something moving and alive in its own right, not fixed and flat and bound like the colouring of a map, grew gradually stronger.... But though I could know, in retrospect, that the changing world seemed nearer the true quality of experience, to give oneself to this knowledge seemed like taking some dangerous plunge; to part of my mind the changing world seemed near to a mad one and the fixed world the only sanity.

Immersing yourself in sensory experience can heighten acuity, but when experience becomes too heightened or is enhanced by emotion, it can slip into visual, auditory, tactile, or olfactory hallucination.

The other muse on the library steps is a painter. Instead of a celestial globe, she grips a palette and clutch of brushes that look like sprigs of asparagus. Her neck leans forward but her head turns back, as if she were looking at something, or had stopped to talk to someone who'd entered the room behind her. Her eyes are wide, rather than lidded like her sister's, and her nostrils are slightly flared as if to take in as much breath as possible. The paintbrush in her hand is tipped with gold.

The shadow behind the door

Fear is a regular companion of those who stake their lives on creating something from nothing. "No one starts a creative endeavor without a certain amount of fear", observes Tharp, "the key is to learn how to keep free-floating fears from paralyzing you before you've begun". Tharp identifies her strongest fears as: "People will laugh at me; I have nothing to say; I will upset someone I love; someone has done it before, and once executed the idea will never be as good as it is in my mind." To her list I would add several fears of my own, including not being believed, not being able to complete what I've started, and letting down those to whom I've committed myself. Not surprisingly, fear also figures prominently in mental illnesses such panic disorders, avoidance disorders, borderline personality disorder, phobias, stress disorders, and depression.

Daughters of memory

Inside the Boston Public Library beside the door to the great reading room, four muses half-walk, half-fly across a grassy meadow. One carries a sprig of laurel and a tiny lyre; the others hold larger versions of ancient harp-guitar instruments with four strings and raise leafed branches – a visual reminder of their role in uniting god(dess), music (the human voice and hands) and the natural world (the branches held aloft). They are clothed in white – the heftier ones held aloft by clouds or cloud-like-wings – and wear laurel wreaths about their heads. On the other side of the door, five more muses holding guitar-harps raise their instruments or laurel sprigs and waft toward a young man with arms held high over the door. A note in the corner of the mural reads "Puvis de Chavannes, '95".

Before written works were available, stories were conveyed through metrical speech, and the Muses were thought to be the source of all knowledge. The early trio of Greek Muses were referred to as *Melete* ("practice"), *Mneme* ("memory"), and *Aiode* ("song"). Their names signify essential elements of creative expression – discipline and practice; memory and imagination; and the transfer of understanding made possible by combining the rhythmic cadences of the heartbeat, breath, and human voice, with knowledge of the world. As conservators of all knowledge, the ancient poets were often called upon to recite for many hours. They apparently managed this feat by entering trance-like states in which they extemporized on well-known tales while relying on a deep familiarity with meter.

Hesiod's *Theogony*, written in the seventh or eighth century BCE, is the first known work to identify nine Muses by the names we associate with them, and to assign to each an art form such as epic poetry, history, sacred music, or dance. Their differentiation was superficial, however, for the Muses continued to be described as being "all of one mind", perhaps because different art forms share a common creative process. In some places, all nine were referred to simply as "*Mneiae*" or "Remembrances" – an acknowledgment of the centrality of memory in art and knowledge.

I laid the fragile, crumbling yellowed newspaper article out on the table before me, glancing around the vault-like room on the third floor of the library where rare books and manuscripts are kept, and lifted the filmy tissue that separated the news article from a delicate, 100-year-old note penned in elegant swirling letters. "With the permission of the Boston Public Library trustees, Architect Charles McKim has approached Pierre Puvis de Chavannes about painting the mural for the first large free public library in the nation." Underneath the next slip of tissue paper, McKim envisions this new library to be a "palace of the people".

I can tell McKim badly wants Puvis de Chavannes to do the murals in the new library: he has given him carte blanche over the grandest hall in the building – eight arched spaces above the grand marble staircase, and the 600-foot wall separating the great reading room from the marble hall. He's offered Puvis almost double what the painter received for murals in the Pantheon and the Sorbonne. McKim makes a special trip to Paris to remind Puvis that Boston believes his murals at museums in Lyon and Amiens are unsurpassed by any other living artist. But Puvis, already in his late 60s, is reluctant to agree to decorate a building he has not seen and probably will never see.

The word "remember" comes through Old French from the Latin words for "think again" (*re* + *memorari*), but "member" can also refer to a limb of the body. We recall facts, but our most vivid memories are those that we re-experience in our bodies. Such involuntary sensory memories can be summoned by the smell of freshly cut grass, or the opening notes of a song that transports us to back to the year in which we first heard the song. But for those who suffer panic, or whose vivid sensory memories are linked to fear, anger, or shame, the backfiring of a car, or a certain brand of aftershave lotion can rekindle terror.

Writers conjure sensory details from memory and imagination, simulating a story's effect within themselves to create images and scenes. But when the background awareness that reminds a writer that such simulated events aren't "real" grows too faint, the writer can find himself descending into the darkness of his characters' conflicts. If the simulated emotion is compounded by present emotional stress in the writer's current life – such as a fear of failing – the merging of the simulated and the real can be compelling.

There is another kind of memory that artists sometimes refer to as "contextual" memory. Contextual memory is born from the amalgam of subtle cues and impressions that normally ride below conscious awareness. Writers visit the locations in which their stories are set and research topics that will never appear on the page in order to build the contextual memory that vivifies experience. Most of the time contextual knowledge is taken for granted, but it can emerge into consciousness with attention, or when the observer or environment undergoes drastic change. In the fearful or traumatized, attention plus heightened contextual memory goes by the name of hyper-vigilance.

When Homer and the other ancient Greek poets composed multi-hour epic narratives, they were drawing on centuries of oral history and folklore and the call-and- response of meter and pattern known as "ancient" or "ancestral" memory. Ancestral memory experiences are not unusual today, but they seem mysterious and mystical (and therefore less real) because the recollector feels that she is accessing memory of a time and place in which she was not physically present. "We believe our ancestors are watching us, even if we do not see them", Cambodian dancer Sina Koy tells *The New York Times.* "It was because of the spirits of the ancestors inside me that I became a dancer." "When you learn a language", observed author Aldous Huxley, "you are an inheritor of the wisdom of the people who have gone before you".

I am fluent only in English, but I've spent a lot of time playing with words, and I'm amazed at how often what I am struggling to say but do not yet fully comprehend is lodged in original root meanings of words that my intellect questions, but some subterranean murmuring urges me not to discard. A visual artist friend who's had similar experiences in museums believes that the feeling of familiarity, déjà vu, or instant recognition that is the hallmark of ancient memory may be a subconscious recognition of pattern. When we consciously or unconsciously seek confirmation or greater understanding of self, our unconscious may recognize a posture, form, or pattern in some person, object, or landscape that echoes or completes a thread of understanding in us essential to who we are or the task at hand.

Artist Puvis de Chavannes has protested that the architect for the new library is asking him to create a series of murals "without having studied the setting, lighting, the general aspects of things", and assures McKim that, despite the money, the proposed project is impossible. From scraps of a letter so faded, I can barely pick out every third word, I gather that McKim is sending an emissary to Paris with a model cast of the library. Puvis de Chavennes says he is too busy working on a mural for Paris City Hall, but writes to one of his students, "The architect has sent me an ambassador with such instructions, such absolute submission, such liberty for myself, that to refuse would be brutal. What is one to say to a man who tells you, 'we will wait ten years for you and longer if necessary – we will wait as long as you like?' In vain I showed my white beard, nothing was of any avail. On Friday morning I am to go and see a little plaster model of the building made specially for me. I shall have to think it over."

Turning the strange familiar and the familiar strange

Artists and writers call upon facts, fictions, and feelings stored away in memory and find new ways to connect them to the world. Another term for this is metaphor. "Metaphor", writes Tharp, "is the lifeblood of all art, if it is not art itself". For Cynthia Ozick, "Metaphors transform the strange into the familiar. This is the rule even of the simplest metaphor – Homer's wine-dark sea for example. 'If you know wine,' says the image, 'you will know the sea.'"

Even when writers are not explicitly using metaphor, they are thinking metaphorically – that is, they seek to translate their own or another's experience into language that will evoke the feelings and meaning of that experience in an audience. Scrutinizing perceptual and emotional nuances and their interconnections and conflicts – especially when using your own body as a sounding board – can amplify any predispositional sensitivity. Concert pianist Hephzibah Menuhin describes her sensitivity:

> My mother would read to us from Dickens and Tolstoy. I remember the scene of the man being beaten in Resurrection and how much it affected me. I didn't understand the plot or who he was politically, only that he was somebody who was being beaten and that I felt it very strongly. In 1934 I came across a book which had been smuggled out of Germany during the Nazi period, showing the scars on people's bodies from beatings. All of the events seemed connected to each other.

Although we often hear about the wonders of connection, there is also a price. Those who are acutely attuned to feeling connected are also keenly aware of disconnection. Disconnection typically leads to or results from internal or external conflict, so sensitivity to connection and disconnection enhances an awareness of conflict. "One pays a lot for awareness", observes poet Audre Lorde. "When I develop that sense of awareness, I develop, by extension a sense concerning you…. I may have to fight you, but as soon as I am aware of you, I must relate to you. I must take you in." The Muses may gift us with story, but stories involve conflict. One of the things that writers and the emotionally distressed have in common is that they spend most of their days thrashing about in conflict even when nothing seems to be going on.

Three years after Charles McKim returned from Paris, Puvis de Chavennes relented at last. With great excitement the library trustees informed the Mayor of Boston: "[T]he most distinguished living mural artist has hitherto refused to work outside of France, believing that his talent should be devoted to his native country, but his well-known admiration for America has induced him for once to break the rule that he has laid down for himself and consent to do for Boston what he has refused to do for any other city or government."

In the next fragment of yellowed correspondence, Puvis, now 70 years old, has begun work on a mural of the "inspiring muses" in his studio in Neuilly, France. In addition to erecting a 60-foot wall with a 2-story door in the center to replicate the Boston library space, he has made architectural models of the grand staircase and the arched loggia that opens onto the mural wall and has requested samples of the Italian marble that is being cut for the staircase, columns, and second floor hall. He sketches hundreds of life drawings using live models, distilling the images and framing them up, before he realizes that his Muses will have to fly over the mural meadow or they will appear to patrons ascending the staircase to be truncated at the waist by the second floor balustrade. "I am working hard at my Boston", he writes to a pupil a year later, "and am advancing very slowly. The impossibility of knowing a thousand details of the entourage [surroundings], a thousand really necessary things is truly terrible".

Beyond our conscious control

In early Greece, the Muses were thought to plant in the mortal poet's mind the events that he was about to relate and to confer upon him the gift of song, giving gracefulness to his words. Later Greek poets invoked a Muse at the beginning of an epic story to guide the teller. As works were written down and could be studied, copied, and revised, the notion of the Muse using the poet as a ventriloquist's doll evolved into the belief that a Muse could gift an already highly skilled artist with inspiration. "Inspire" and "spirit" are derived from the Latin *spiritus*, meaning "breath" – the animating principle in animals and man that originally included both the god-given and emotional aspects of a person. Inspiration as breath is an apt metaphor: besides being essential to life, breathing is controlled

DOI: 10.1057/9781137381668

by the unconscious autonomic nervous system and is also somewhat subject to conscious control.

Nineteenth-century Romantic poets such as Samuel Taylor Coleridge and Percy Bysshe Shelley claimed that artists were exceptional beings gifted with inspiration by being attuned to "divine mystical winds" and having sensitive souls able to receive visions. Sigmund Freud claimed that inspiration sprang from unresolved psychological conflict and childhood trauma within the artist's inner psyche. Carl Gustav Jung suggested that artists are particularly attuned to *memory*, which carries the *archetypes* of the human mind and are, therefore, more sensitive to the universal. In the late-twentieth and early-twenty-first century, inspiration, once attributed to the daughters of Memory, has been recast as unconscious "primary processing", "pre-logical thought", or "bio-associative thinking". The one thing that everyone seems to agree on is that inspiration is beyond conscious control. What then separates inspiration from madness?

Inspiration versus possession

In *Phaedrus* Plato equated inspiration with divine madness:

> Madness, provided it comes from heaven, is the channel by which we receive the greatest blessings. [A]ccording to our ancestors, madness is a nobler thing than sober sense…. Madness comes from God whereas sober sense is merely human.

However, those who suffer from madness, including many artists and writers, often do not find it an ennobling experience. The boundary between being inspired and being taken hostage by illness appears to be defined by three markers: whether the person retains some mediating awareness of her "normal" self and her surroundings; and, if so, whether the person is able to exert some level of control over herself and the experience; and whether something productive is generated from the altered state.

In *The Act of Creation,* Arthur Koestler describes the importance of maintaining mediating awareness and some agency while in an altered state:

> We have seen that the creative act always involves a regression to earlier, more primitive levels in the hierarchy [of mental processing], while other processes continue simultaneously on the rational surface – a condition

that reminds one of a skin diver with a breathing tube.... The capacity to regress, more or less at will, to the games of the underground, without losing contact with the surface, seems to be the essence of the poetic, and any other form of creativity.

Apparently, the Greeks also recognized the need for the artist to maintain contact with the rational; Apollo, god of reason, was the leader of the Muses.

For sustained artistic production, access to both the unconscious and rational thought appears to be necessary, but the interplay between them can take different forms. Some artists experience inspiration as a fiery tumult with "cool headed" reason showing up late in the process. Composer Peter Tchaikovsky wrote to a colleague, that "[A] sense of bliss...comes over me [when] a new idea awakens in me.... I forget everything and behave like a mad man. Everything within me starts pulsing and quivering...." Others describe inspiration as dipping in and out of a deep pool or the bubbling up of an underground spring. In *The Name and Nature of Poetry*, A. E. Housman details one of his daily walks:

> As I went along, thinking of nothing in particular, only looking at things around me and following the progress of the seasons, there would flow into my mind, with sudden and unaccountable emotion, sometimes a line or two of verse, sometimes a whole stanza at once, accompanied, not preceded, by a vague notion of the poem in which they were destined to form a part. Then there would be a lull of an hour or so, then perhaps the spring would bubble up again. I say bubble up, because, as far as I could make out, the source of the suggestions thus proffered to the brain was an abyss...the pit of my stomach. When I got home I wrote them down, leaving gaps, and hoping that further inspiration might be forthcoming another day.

Novelist Italo Calvino describes a process of poking around for an idea, seeing what arises, puttering with images and arrangements, and trying to recognize a good result without having any real moment-to-moment knowledge of how he got from A to B:

> Think, for instance, of a writer who is trying to convey certain ideas which to him are contained in mental images. He isn't quite sure how those images fit together in his mind, and he experiments around, expressing things first one way and then another, and finally settles on some version. But does he know where it all came from? Only in a vague sense. Much of the source, like an iceberg, is deep underwater, unseen – and he knows that.

Even the "cooler" forms of inspiration can produce intense emotion and lead to mental and emotional exhaustion. In the intensified process of attending, amplifying, and refining emotional, sensory, and intellectual content – together with whatever stress the artist himself brings to the project (deadlines, fear of not being able to make the project work, commitments to other people, and so forth) – the boundary between inspiration and insanity can blur.

Great distress and incoherency often precede great coherency, and once the fruit has been harvested, it is easy to forget the process. However, some states, particularly those from which the sufferer is not confident of return, are so distressing that a productive outcome may be unimportant. While in college, I worked for a short time as a movie reviewer. In addition to going to classes, I often saw three or four movies a week, sitting down immediately afterward to write reviews that were due to my editors within 48 hours. I soon discovered that I could recall more if, instead of trying to mentally tag events as important as I watched the films, I simply "opened myself up" and absorbed as wholly as possible what was unfolding in front of me. But I soon reached a physical, mental, and emotional saturation point which I realized only after I went to see *The Exorcist* and started hallucinating in philosophy class the next day. I spent the weekend in a dim, quiet infirmary room learning to control vivid, terrifying images – leering faces, eyes jetting fire, and shrieks of ridiculing laughter – that I knew weren't real but was convinced could annihilate me. I couldn't look at people's faces, for whenever I detected the slightest trace of critical judgment, the horrors returned. After a few days, I was able to return to class, but for years a jeering specter could materialize if I got into a heated argument with someone I cared about. I became adept at jerking my head away from the trigger and slipping into another room until the image subsided. Over time, I recognized the shadowing in my peripheral vision and the grab in my ribcage that preceded a vision and could move to avoid it, but 30 years later I am still careful not to look at movie trailers that too closely resemble the original catalyst. I learned some things from the experience (including the fact that the human mind cannot be pushed indefinitely), but I do not think of it as creative. My mind and every other fiber of my body recoiled in order to survive, whereas inspiration – as quixotic and painful as it can be – always bends toward life.

The longing to belong

Artists and those who suffer from mental illness are often palpably aware of being different. "I've always been aware that something in my life was not quite right, if not totally wrong", writes Meri Nana-Ama Danquah. "My scales were never balanced. For every twelve joys, I had twenty-five sorrows. And each sorrow was like a song." The mentally distressed and the artistic may be particularly attuned to difference because it often creates internal conflict, an aching that can't be soothed, or a generalized sense of discomfort. Poet Audre Lorde remembers feeling at odds with her family as a young child without being able to identify why:

> I was a very difficult child. I was a rebel from the time I can remember and I can remember fairly far back. My earliest memories are of war between Me and Them. "Them" were my two sisters and my parents. It was their camp against mine, and since there were always more of them, I knew very early that I would have to be smarter than all of them put together. I don't know exactly how I knew this, but I did. This was in New York, in Manhattan, in the middle of Harlem on 142nd Street and Lenox Avenue.

Surrealist painter Leonor Fini describes a similar feeling born of a different circumstance:

> I grew up in a cultivated bourgeois house, but "culture" was something that was meant to stay in books or on the table. It was never conceived as something that penetrates and actually becomes the person herself. As soon as I began painting what was in my head, the people around me were shocked.... I wanted to integrate the "culture" that surrounded me with my own universe inside. I always imagined I would have a life very different from the one that was imagined for me, but I understood from a very early time that I would have to revolt in order to have that life.

In addition to being sensitive to connection and disconnection and aware of feeling different – or perhaps because of it – artists and people with mood disorders tend to be particularly concerned with their place in the world. Making peace with one's place in the world can be more difficult for artists and the ill than for others. The ill often define "the world" as a place far from their palpable experience – a world that may include their former "healthy" self, other people who appear to be leading normal or easier lives, or others' definitions of healthy behavior. Writers and artists who spend their lives creating works for people they don't know tend to define the community against which they measure themselves, or the place in which they hope to have impact, as very large in time in space (such as, "beginning with Shakespeare and extending to eternity", or "all those who live in poverty and cannot speak for themselves"). As playwright Fay Weldon observes, "creative writing which tries to make sense of the universe or of yourself... is quite painful in a way. It can make you distraught. I daresay it ought to if you are doing it properly".

Writers and those suffering from depression and other mental illnesses also frequently share a preoccupation with life and death. For the depressed, death or suicide can represent escape from pain that the sufferer isn't sure he can tolerate, or is sure he can't tolerate and isn't sure is going to end, or is sure isn't going to end. Being preoccupied with whether you are going to live or die makes every other decision, success, or disappointment relatively unimportant. It offers temporary relief from whatever is disturbing you because nothing matters until you decide you're going to live. Eventually, to keep the body interested in the debate you begin to ask yourself, not whether you will live or die, but when and how you will make the move. "I built up to the act carefully and for a long time, with a kind of blank pertinacity", writes A. Alvarez in *The Savage God: A Story of Suicide*. "It was the one constant focus of my life, making everything else irrelevant, a diversion. Each sporadic burst of work, each minor success and disappointment, each moment of calm and relaxation, seemed merely a temporary halt on my steady descent...."

For writers, a preoccupation with life or death is more of an occupation: to draw readers into the author-created world and hold their attention, a reader must feel something critical is at stake. As author Eudora Welty observes:

> What can a character come to know, of himself and others, by working through a given situation?... Any novel's situation must constitute some version of a matter of life or death.... This may or may not be the case in a literal sense; but it does need to be always the case as a matter of spiritual or moral survival. It may lie not so much in being rescued as in having learned what constitutes one's own danger, and one's own salvation.

The suicidal impulse is, in part, a desire to control your destiny when the conscious mind says you can't tolerate any more, but your body continues to breathe and feel and beat. Control over one's own death can feel empowering, especially to those who don't feel in control of much else in their lives. "I could see day after day glaring ahead of me like a white, broad infinitely desolate avenue", wrote Sylvia Plath in her thinly disguised autobiography, *The Bell Jar*. "It seemed silly to wash one day when I would only have to wash the next. It made me tired just to think of it. I wanted to do everything once and for all and be done with it."

In high school, I gravitated toward Eugene O'Neill, Samuel Beckett, and all things existential. I was introduced to Sylvia Plath's poetry by my eleventh-grade English teacher who had been Sylvia Plath's English teacher some 20 years earlier and claimed to have been a mentor. I'd read *The Bell Jar* the year before, but when I studied the poems in *Ariel* I saw, with creeping horror and fascination, what Sylvia Plath had done. I did not exactly understand how the poems had been constructed, but I could see and feel what she had done with her mind. I could smell the edge of danger.

I did not know in high school – nor for a long time thereafter – that despair feels endless, not because it is endless, but because that's what despair is. (If you could see the end, you wouldn't be in despair.) I wanted to lose myself. I wanted to save myself, I wanted to save others. I wanted to be consumed and die for a cause and be rescued. I believed books and writing could do all of this, and I was too impatient to think that carrying water for 50 years could be meaningful. By sacrificing myself to a story, I thought I might finally belong. I wrote a novel and tried to take my life. Sometime after I figured my life would be over, my body realized that my mind wasn't going to help and threw it over. When I regained consciousness in the hospital, I did not know how to succeed at living, but I knew that my body did not want to die. I would never again doubt its intentions.

In the second-floor library stairwell, opposite the 60-foot mural of the "inspiring muses", long panels depict Homer, Socrates, and the play by Aeschylus in which the sirens arrogantly challenge the Muses to a music contest and lose their feathers. On the west wall, beyond the panels of Homer and Aeschylus, a pale muse glides horizontally, clutching her laurel sprig. Below the light muse, a dark twin glides on the other's slipstream, her hand covering her face with fingers spread just wide enough to peek through. Beneath them – weirdly out of time for these turn-of-the-century fresco-like paintings – a six-limbed electric power line, strung with high-tension wires, stands on the hillside. In the rare manuscript vault I discover that the panel on the west well symbolizes the future. What I thought were high-tension wires are telegraph wires – communication. But the future is both light and dark.

Limits and wholeness

The word "create" comes from the Latin word, *creare*, meaning "to rise", "to grow", "to make". Creativity pushes toward life. But life includes death, so perhaps it is more accurate to say that creativity pushes toward wholeness. Even though art can be commercially devalued, it will always be with us, for art is as close as humans can come to representing the whole of our experience. But there can never be a complete or perfect representation of life because life is predicated on movement. In movement there can be unity and completion, but never for more than a moment. So there is frustration. Imperfection crops up at every turn. Our lives are limited: our patience, resources, health, abilities, attention, strength – everything is limited. When the limits on our perceptions, emotions, or associational thinking become too loose, we are unable to manage. When we simulate others' limits within ourselves, the potential for experiencing life in all its parts and wholeness is immense, overwhelming, exciting, and fraught.

In Aeschylus' lost play *Bassarides*, Dionysius, god of ecstasy and excess, feels slighted by Orpheus, the gifted mortal musician and son of muse Calliope. He sends his devotees, the Bassarai, to harass Orpheus. The Bassarai, known for frenzied ecstasies that frequently erupt into violence, tear Orpheus to pieces and scatter his limbs. The Muses are grief-stricken. Although immortal, they cannot breathe life into dead mortals. Orpheus' lyre is placed in the night sky, and the Muses gather up the pieces of Orpheus and bury them together while composing a lament. But Orpheus' lyre cannot play itself; art requires a mortal.

Part of my journey has been learning to see vivid images and dark despair as my body's inarticulate attempt to help me, rather than as a terrible unchosen affliction. The feeling-image that seems like a hindrance often turns out to be the key to some daunting problem, although it's sometimes hard to see, especially if I don't want to listen. For the ancients and many contemporary artists, a Muse can function as an inspiring guide or guardian when passing between the conscious and the unconscious, the personal and the universal, the literal and the envisioned, or the "given" and the discipline of "practice". A Muse can also house and safeguard an artist's deepest aspirations, longings, and fears while reinforcing his or her desire for relationship with an "other".

De Chavennes' 60-foot mural, *Le Muses inspiratrices acclamant le Genie messager de lumiere*, was finished in time to be exhibited at the French Salon in 1895. Five of the eight panels were exhibited in 1896, and the remaining three were shown at the Durand-Ruel Galleries before they too were sent to America. De Chavennes, who'd devoted three years to his Muses, was reluctant to see them leave for Boston. "Never again, shall I accept such a task", he mourned, "I am like a father whose daughters are leaving him for a convent".

The mentally ill may or may not have a desire to authentically communicate with the world; the artist nearly always seeks authentic exchange with others, although the exchange sought may be a relationship between her work and an audience rather than a relationship between the artist and audience. The writer or artist may be an outsider, but through his or her art, he seeks to be represented and accepted at least by proxy into the human fold. In representing what is missing from our current discourse, or by creating a new whole that reconciles previously conflicting feelings and ideas, art becomes the Muse's dream of unifying past and future, known and unknown, the momentary and the eternal.

Works cited

Alvarez, A. "From *The Savage God*". Rpt. *Unholy Ghost; Writers on Depression*. Ed. Casey, Nell. New York: Perennial, 2002. Print. 214–215.
Barron, Frank, Alfono Montuori, and Anthea Barron, eds *Creators on Creating; Awakening and Cultivating the Imaginative Mind*. New York: Jeremy P. Tarcher/Putnam, 1997. Print. Interviews: Italo Calvino 101, Marion Milner, 113–114, Peter Ilyich Tchaikovsky 180–181.
Danquah, Meri Nana-Ama. "Writing the Wrongs of Identity". *Unholy Ghost; Writers on Depression*. Ed. Casey, Nell. New York: Perennial, 2002. Print. 174–175.
Hensick, Teri, Kate, Oliver, and Pocobene, Gianfranco. "Puvis de Chavennes's Allegorical Murals in the Boston Public Library: History, Technique, and Conservation". *Journal of the American Institute for Conservation*, 1997. 36(1). Print.
Homer. *Iliad: The Fitzgerald Translation*. New York: Macmillan, 2004. 531.
Huxley, Aldous. *The Perennial Philosophy*. Harper Perennial, 1990. Print.
Koestler, Arthur. *The Act of Creation*. New York: Macmillan, 1965. Print. 316–317.

McKim, Charles Follen. "Correspondence of Charles Follen McKim 1847–1909". Courtesy of the Trustees of the Boston Public Library/ Rare Books. Boston: Boston Public Library Rare Books and Manuscripts. 8 August 2012. Print.

Plath, Sylvia. *The Bell Jar.* New York: Perennial Classics, 1999. Print. 143.

Plato. *Symposium* and *Phaedrus.* New York: Dover Publications, 1993. Print. 59–60.

Tharp, Twyla. *The Creative Habit; Learn It and Use It for Life.* New York: Simon & Schuster, 2003. Print. Tharp 5; Ozick 64; and Koy 68.

Welty, Eudora. *On Writing.* New York: Modern Library, 2002. Print. 98.

Winter, Nina. *Interview with the Muse; Remarkable Women Speak on Creativity and Power.* California: Moon Books, 1978. Print. Interviews: Leonor Fini 57, Audre Lorde 74, Hephzibah Menuhin 101–2, and Fay Weldon 42.

3
After the Fire Goes Out: Writing before and after Treatment for an Affective Disorder

Lise Bagoley

Abstract: *For "Lise", "publishing this under my own name is too great a risk for an early career academic, so I have chosen to use a pseudonym; although I hope this essay will help others living and writing with depression and bipolar disorder, what motivated me was the opportunity to write about both the nadir of my struggle and the way my disease continues to impact my life after treatment. I am beginning to make sense of how being bipolar shapes my life". In the quiet rush of joy that is hypomania, Lise feels "like an open faucet, words pouring out... I remember things from years ago with great clarity.... I take in everything". But a single experience of true mania – of psychosis – prompted this writer to seek treatment, with diverse implications for her craft.*

Keywords: Hypomania; mania; bipolar disorder; psychosis; treatment; writers

Horton, Stephanie Stone, ed. *Affective Disorder and the Writing Life: The Melancholic Muse*. Basingstoke: Palgrave Macmillan, 2014. DOI: 10.1057/9781137381668.

It's 2 a.m. on a Friday night, and I am wide awake. This isn't unusual for me. I adored the college party scene, and partied at every opportunity. What was unusual: this is Friday night, and I'm in my apartment doing schoolwork, writing to beat the band. Although a dedicated student, like many of my peers, I devoted equal time to play, and I never missed a weekend night out (or, admittedly, a weeknight). I wasn't content to give up parties for study, or vice versa. I took pride in this, and I failed to reckon honestly the toll this lifestyle took on me – long days overtired, dehydrated, and jumpy; blood pumping caffeine and nicotine through my body as I fought to stay awake; promises to myself that I would cut back, get some rest tonight. But then came the inevitable – the party or show that simply couldn't be missed. I'd get a renewed burst of energy and do it all over again. Yet on this Friday, in my last semester of undergraduate work, my senior thesis – two "long short stories" – kept me happily at home, sober, and working.

The words flowed easily that spring. They often struck me blocks from home, full sentences unfolding as I cut across the park in Dupont Circle or climbed the stairs of the Metro. They astonished me sometimes. My advisor was surprised at how quickly I had written the stories as well as by their quality. Surely, much of this jump in quality was attributable to her good tutelage and the heavy dose of reading (and hence the plethora of models) assigned by my literature professors. Yet something had changed. I could stroke my ego and say it was hard work, but the truth is that it rarely seemed like work.

My renewed dedication took some of my friends aback. Perhaps they noticed what I have heard therapists call a "sudden personality change". In truth, the high I got from writing was better than any I could obtain at the crowded parties abundant on and near campus. When I hit a stopping point that night, at 2 a.m., I thought about checking out a party, but instead I did what seemed to me a perfectly logical thing to do: I laced up a pair of roller skates, pushed my way down the hall of our carpeted condominium building, fled through the lobby before the security guard could stop me, and propelled myself out into the night. Spring had come early to the District, and the famous cherry blossoms popped against the night sky, electrifying pink. The air was sweet with pollen. I was overcome by a rush of total well-being. After a few quick laps around my block, I turned onto a brick-paved street lined with large, artfully restored townhomes. As I picked up speed and turned at the dead-end, I could see several lights click on in second-floor windows. I zoomed up the street one last time and headed home, where I continued to write until the river of words stopped flowing around 4 a.m.

From experience, I know there is a sizable grain of truth in the myth of the mad writer. In the hypomanic (mild mania) stage of bipolar I disorder, words flow effortlessly. Hypomania can be extremely productive, and hence extremely seductive. This is why I didn't seek psychiatric counsel for four years after graduating from college, though those delightfully productive streaks were short-lived, and the increasingly deep troughs of depression that dominated my winters nearly disabled me. Once that initial hypomania receded, I never finished those two stories to my liking. I tinkered with the endings for a while with less than satisfactory results. With the encouragement of some writer/teachers who had seen my work at its best, I applied to several MFA programs. To my disappointment, I was accepted by only one, and I did not receive the financial assistance I needed to attend. I decided to start on an MA in literature instead. I stowed those stories away in a box.

Am I incapable of writing well without the spur of such seemingly divine inspiration? Years ago, I thought this to be true; now I know it is not. Had my bipolar illness been limited to periods of hypomania and depression, I may never have discovered this fact, but when I experienced a severe manic episode (true mania) four years later, I made the decision to begin treatment.

Last July, I attended my last appointment with a psychiatrist in Providence. It had been nine years almost to the date from my second and last hospitalization. Like a lot of early-career academics, I move often, and was headed to Pittsburgh, Pennsylvania. I had been fortunate to find a physician in Rhode Island who listened to my concerns carefully, without the condescension I occasionally experienced. She took care to revisit my diagnosis and rule out the possibility that my manic episodes were caused by other mitigating factors, like substance abuse or being overmedicated for depression. She concluded soundly that I have a true bipolar I disorder. She offered to give me the records from my hospitalizations, which were obtained with much bureaucratic difficulty. As a writer and as a person, I was curious – these were the record of the most confusing and frightening days of my life. Nonetheless, I declined her offer. "I would be tempted to read them", I told her. "It would be too upsetting."

Revisiting these events from my own point of view has been jarring enough. In an attempt to stroke my ego, I could say that I am delving into them for an altruistic reason – to help others. Critics of the recent spate of memoirs and recovery narratives may suggest quite the opposite – that chapters like this are exercises in navel-gazing, or, worse, trading upon the morbid curiosity of others for our own financial and professional gain. To the contrary, publishing this chapter under my own name is too great a risk for an early-career academic, so I have chosen to use a pseudonym; although I hope this chapter will help others living and writing with depression and bipolar disorder. What motivated me was the opportunity to write about both the nadir of my struggle and the way my disease continues to impact my life after treatment. I am beginning to make sense of how being bipolar shapes my life – particularly my working life. I do this with the knowledge that seminal books on creativity and bipolar disorder have helped many, both those with and without affective disorders, to understand the case for a link between creative work and affective disorders. What I do hope is that through my chapter, readers may begin to understand (or identify with) both the opportunities and the obstacles presented by treatment for those disorders, something that I am just beginning to understand myself.

As so much has been made of the link between bipolar disorder and creativity, the most important thing I want to say is that the "productive phase" I describe above only tells *part* of the story for someone with bipolar I. Yes, hypomania is wonderful. The barriers between me and everything else – the past, others, the sensory world – completely melt. A friend once said that when he was depressed, he felt brittle. Having experienced many bouts of depression, I think this is apt. When I am hypomanic, by contrast, I feel extremely porous. I can remember things from years ago with great clarity. I empathize fully with others. The scent of the air and its feel on my skin seems to infuse me with an almost electric charge. I take in everything.

At some point, this wonderful hypomania cedes to a more intense high that makes it tempting to live on the surface, rather than to delve deeply into the world as creative and academic writers must. As I move out of the productive phase, my imagination is still in overdrive, but I cannot pause long enough to sort out my musings. I am driven by a bottomless craving for more of everything. I move forward and forward and forward. I shop. I say a lot, but feel very little. Life is happy and uncomplicated as a pop hit by Katy Perry. Everything glitters and it is all gold. Everyone is beautiful. Desires are as permanent as a shiny bubble. Life is as sweet as a bottomless cherry Slurpee and no more nourishing.

I drink it all up, and I am thirstier still. I talk and talk and talk, more and better than usual. I am usually shy, but I become irreverent and make people laugh. I soon see that I am funnier than I actually am. I begin to speak so quickly that I become hard to follow. I never literally believe I am invincible, that I can fly, for example. Instead, I become utterly careless, too focused on what's next and next and next to lock the door or to look behind me when I reverse my car. I lose sight of responsibilities and instead spend hours on distractions like reality television, that normally have little appeal.

When I shift up another gear into psychosis (this has happened twice), I feel an urgent drive not so much to write, but to communicate. Just as I do in the most fertile periods of hypomania, I feel I am blessed with a heavy dose of insight. The difference is that my insights are patently false. I find myself saturated with information. At first, this information is a tangled mess, but my mind works overtime sorting this input and concludes that everything is connected. Hence, the paranoid delusions begin. As I do in the most fertile periods of mania, I feel like an open faucet, words pouring out. For someone who has never had such an experience, a loss of sanity might seem to be a breakdown of logic. For me, it is logic on overdrive. Every fleeting thought has importance and must be woven into the web, traced back to a cause. When my moods suddenly and intermittently turn dark, I become convinced that these feelings have a root in reality, and I trace them back to what I believe was the certain fact of a miserable childhood. I had never been happy (I had not been a popular kid by any means, but there were many pictures of me smiling genuine smiles). We moved around a lot (I moved only three times by the age of 18). There had been much yelling and screaming at home (fights were rare). I never had any friends (although my friendships often faded, I was never without a best friend, sometimes two). I didn't have a "good" family (my family is as untouched by strife as any I know; at this time, my parents had been together for 25 years, and even in my extended family, there were no long-standing feuds). My parents were not my biological parents (any stranger could look at our features and sort out our relationship). They didn't love me (they did, and they were terrified by what was happening to me).

My parents tried patiently to dispel my delusions. At one point, my mom offered me some money. She knew I was broke. I was in many ways an average 20-something, at least in the sense that I indulged in luxuries at every opportunity with little eye toward saving for the future. On most days, offering me $20 to cheer me up might have been a reasonable thought. What did I think instead? She is trying to buy me off. Shut me up. She urged me to let them take me to the emergency room. I ultimately let them, not because they asked me but despite of it. I did not distrust my thoughts, but I could no longer stand the assault they launched on my mind. The hospital staff became my parents' co-conspirators. The doctors and other health care workers were trying to get me to admit something, I suspected, some terrible fact or crime I was sure I was suspected of, even though I couldn't settle on exactly what it was. I thought this was why different clinicians repeated the same questions many times during my intake and evaluation. I also interpreted the fact that I was seen by hospital workers of varying ages, genders, races, and ethnicities, some of whom worked alone and some of whom worked in pairs, as the hospital's attempt to psych me out. I thought the repetition of the questions – the differing styles of questioning, and the use of different inquirers – was a ploy to get me to confess to something (I must have picked this up from my love of cop shows). It was decided I was going to be sent to a unit for the high functioning. I didn't feel I fit this description at all. They called it the "atrium", and promised it was the best place in the hospital. I assumed my mother had paid them off, and I declined their offer. They changed their plans, and sent me to the dual-diagnosis floor. I concluded they changed their plans because I had called attention to the bribe.

During my hospital stay, the delusions faded only to be replaced by alternating periods of stupor and anxiety. I was instructed not to live alone for weeks or to drive for months – with good reason. The pills made me utterly lethargic. My average day was split evenly between sleeping and being awake. Whether it was overmedication or depression and anxiety that followed on the heels of mania, it made for an unproductive streak. Although many readers might assume this is another case of a too-cautious physician overmedicating a patient, I clung to that treatment like a life raft. Some minor slip-ups showed me that despite the side effects, I could not be without it.

For example, in an effort to revamp my admittedly unhealthy habits, I began visiting the gym. On the day I was photographed for my membership card, I had forgotten my morning dose of risperdone. The worker operating the camera politely showed me my first photograph, which revealed my eyes looking suspiciously out of my peripheral vision, and asked me if I wanted to retake the photo. I was not literally afraid of those around me – an improvement from the eye of the storm – but my thoughts, my eyes, and my heart were racing nonetheless, and tremors began. It was clear that holistic measures like jogging and swimming would do nothing for these severe symptoms without medication.

I returned to my studies a month later, with a break from teaching responsibilities. The wisdom of returning so quickly was questionable. My 12-waking-hour day consisted almost entirely of make-up work. Every task was labored, completed while curled in bed because of my absolute intolerance for being even slightly uncomfortable in a drafty old apartment or with anxious trembling eased only by the cigarette I allowed myself to smoke every 15 minutes.

I tried to study for my master's exam. Once, I reread a text that I had already studied, having forgotten that I had already made notes for the exam before my breakdown. My new attempt at a study guide paled next to one I had completed early in the term. Understanding on the most basic level was present – the new plot summary almost replicated the first – but the analysis, the outline of what might become an answer to an essay question, completely lacked in insight.

Recovering my ability to speak, read, write, and teach as I once did seemed impossible, so I dropped out of school with no intention to return. I learned, however, that working a "normal" job without many intellectual demands was not a surefire cure. I experienced a second (albeit less severe) breakdown after trying to jettison treatment in order to recover the energy and spark I so wanted to reclaim. I resumed my ability to function more quickly this time, and my department was fair-minded in readmitting me to complete my master's degree and then enroll in the PhD program. I was grateful, and I wanted desperately to be the student I once was. Learning to work without the spark of mania was a challenge. Yet with the memory of my two manic episodes – in which I believed (ardently) that things entirely untrue were true, and shared those beliefs with anyone who would listen to my thought torrents – I still did not trust myself completely.

Bouts of mild to moderate depression intensified my self-doubt. I became too sensitive to criticism, too prone to self-editing, too reluctant to release my work out into the world in the form of a presentation or a publication, or to take solid positions on texts when teaching or learning in the classroom. Even with treatment, I continued to experience the outer limits of depression. I often dwelled in the past. I felt stagnant. I exhumed and dissected every choice I had ever made, pronouncing most of them foolish. "Foolish" was also the label that I slapped on most of my projects.

I am able to write this chapter now only because I have found a way to live and write despite both my disorder and the hazards of treatment. By the time I reentered graduate school, the relapse I had after discontinuing treatment had given me a healthy dose of fear and a willingness to take my medication as prescribed, but I still tried many ways of mitigating the side effect of listlessness. I discarded the advice of both therapists and academic mentors and nurtured many unhealthy habits in an attempt to replicate the sparks of inspiration I received while manic: chain smoking, drinking pots of coffee, and clinging desperately to my night-owl tendencies despite morning obligations.

Not only did these habits bring the health consequences that anyone might reap from such experiments – a persistent cough, a jittery high followed by a crash, a fatigue that made it even more difficult to teach, grade, and attend classes – they also had particularly harsh consequences for me as someone with bipolar disorder. I knew sleep deprivation was a gamble; I never confessed it to my doctors. I had been warned that too many sleepless nights could induce mania. It never happened, perhaps because I took my medication scrupulously; but sleep deprivation, compounding the sedating effect of medication, made it almost impossible to function. I depended on cigarettes to keep me awake during classes and teaching and to prolong the stretch of evening hours I used for writing and planning my course. I also craved the quick jolt of creative energy that sometimes followed a cup of coffee and a cigarette (or two or three). When I finally decided that cigarettes were leaving me too short of both breath and cash, I had tremendous difficulty quitting. The difficulty any smoker faces in breaking this addiction was compounded because I was wary of the mood swings that came with any attempt to quit; I had never quite lost the fear of having another serious manic or depressive episode. Feeling bad sometimes, I have learned, is a part of being human. At the time, however, feeling bad seemed like the beginning of a perilous road that would end on the psych ward – or worse. I quit smoking successfully, but only after two years of effort; I scraped butts from ashtrays, retrieved cigarettes thrown in the trash, and broke many cigarettes, smoking them filterless, stub by stub. In hindsight, my bad habits kept me in need of more medication than I might otherwise have needed as they created the irritability I used them to assuage. More medication, in turn, left me drowsy and uninspired, primed to turn even more readily to cigarettes and caffeine. It was a safer but ultimately costly shadow of the self-medication I practiced with alcohol before treatment.

Next, in an attempt to create a healthier life, I gave myself over completely to "expert" advice. I took my medication as prescribed and rarely voiced my concerns about being overtired and unmotivated. I considered apathy to be "the new normal" because I was extremely grateful to be delivered from the hell of acute mania. I was wary of asking for adjustments, as these experts also drilled into me that bipolar patients are often ill-equipped to judge the gravity of their own condition.

In attempting to stay afloat in graduate school, I turned to the advice of academic mentors, many of whom said to treat my studies like a job, and to "stick my butt in a seat" from at least nine to five. The upside of this approach, my well-intentioned advisors explained, was to rein in the work and allow for periods of rest and recreation, to keep my considerable workload from consuming my life. I found that although I could sometimes squeeze out a few good hours of writing, I spent too much "butt-in-seat" time tinkering with minor revisions, researching, or alas, Facebooking. My failure at the butt-in-seat method led to much self-reproach. Wasn't discipline and delayed gratification the key to success? Were my restlessness and impulsivity – bipolar traits that seemed to stick around after treatment – going to prevent me from completing my degree?

In hindsight, my attempts to live and work with bipolar disorder characteristically swing between two poles – between the desire to negate the disorder and the desire to let it pick me up and toss me where it will, for better or worse. I am now able to take a more moderate approach. I sift through the advice of academic mentors and embrace only what works. The advice of colleagues and therapists that a writing project can be accomplished in daily, hour spurts is one of the best pieces of advice I have received so far.

My ability to delay gratification is admittedly weak. I am no marathon runner, yet I am a heck of a sprinter. When my mood is good, I can always attain a "writing high" within that hour. I can then ride that high as long as it lasts and push easily beyond that hour. If my workload is heavy, I can plan hour-length spurts for several projects throughout the day. One of the best aspects of academia is having some control over my schedule. I don't have to punch in. I can plan to do my most difficult work – writing – at my best time of day, provided that that time isn't 2:00 a.m. If my mood is poor, an hour a day gives me enough discipline to do something, even if I grumble throughout the hour. My ability to make it through an hour – even if I can never make it through eight hours – keeps me from total despair.

Of course, our workloads are such that an hour a day of writing isn't always enough, but I find that if I start my projects as far in advance as possible and if in the final weeks before a project is due I block off longer periods of time for revision, the task gets done, even allowing for a few days on which a bout of melancholy prevents me from picking up the pen or turning on the laptop. Planning far in advance also shortcuts the last-minute anxiety that can be debilitating for a person prone to self-doubt.

I tried this "sprinting" approach despite my misgivings. I used to think that if I didn't "live" with my projects 24 hours a day, that if I didn't dream of things to write and wake up cursing the fact that I could not remember them, then I wasn't truly a writer. While such a mindset led to bursts of productivity, it also contributed to a complete meltdown that forced me to leave the academy for two years. To mix metaphors, this sprinting approach has given me a safe way to "ride the waves" – to work through slumps, to coast the highs, to seek stability (but not stultification), to work diligently (but not incessantly). I have learned to neither impose a false discipline on myself by punching the clock or to seek out the romantic ideal of a wild-haired, sleepless genius scribbling through the night. Neither approach works for me, perhaps because both lend themselves to the isolation that so frequently hobbles academics and which can be completely crippling to a person whose distorted thinking thrives on isolation.

Instead of obsessing over a project or treating writing as a dreadful but necessary chore (like the butt-in-seat approach), I try to live in the middle of academic life and embrace the joys that motivated me to make the many sacrifices necessary to pursue an academic career. I try to direct myself outward instead of in, to stop seeking to be a mad professor – a person whose dishevelment and fatigue reflects self-care as an impediment rather than a gift. In the extreme hubris that some bipolar people have, I used to regard exercise, sleep, and a healthy social life as the tools of mere mortals; I now understand that sacrificing such balance is sacrificing productivity in the long run and that exercise can bring me that same healthy high that my writing "sprints" can.

I embrace the perk that I don't have to sit in a seat for eight hours a day. Though I may work more than eight hours, I have some control over what these hours are. Instead of ruing the fact that I can't leave my job behind, I delight in the fact that my "job" includes not only teaching but learning: listening to the news, visiting a museum, attending colleagues' presentations, and chatting about books. It is true that academics are frequently assessed via oft-debated formulas measuring the relative worth of our scholarship, teaching, and service. Yet if I give myself over completely to worries about my "quantifiable" value, if I deny too many of those pleasures that come from our line of work, I will seek them elsewhere – in less gratifying and more destructive pursuits. Even though I have been sober for ten years, when I allow myself to be overwhelmed by work, I am prone to the addictions of the "reformed", like shopping and food.

In short, I find it best to view my career as a creative vocation, rather than be wholly consumed with concerns about "measurables". I also find, perhaps paradoxically, that I am more productive if I at least partially embrace some of my bipolar traits even when conventional wisdom holds those traits to be defects. At the same time, I also embrace expert advice on self-care, casting aside my former view that exercise and rest will be distractions rather than boons.

Unfortunately, this type of balance and freedom is difficult to achieve in the current academic climate. As I took on a four-course, three-prep load last semester, I found it difficult to follow my own advice, particularly given that the terms of my full-time temporary position dictated that I continue my job search. My time as an adjunct instructor has made me mindful that more than half of my university's English faculty consists of part-time contingent faculty, many of whom taught four or more courses split between two or more universities. These workers had no access to employer-sponsored health insurance; some worked outside jobs in the service sector in order to secure healthcare coverage. These are perilous conditions for all university instructors; they are even more dangerous for workers with affective disorders. Unmanageable workloads and uncertain workplaces only exacerbate the symptoms of affective disorder, even spurring symptoms in some of the previously healthy. Lack of quality, affordable health care can be career ending for those dependent on therapy and/or medication. No matter how dedicated they are to teaching or scholarship, when faced with financial devastation, non-benefitted faculty may decide to pursue alternative employment.

Much has been written about how universities' unethical employment practices hamper the quality of education, despite adjunct faculty members' considerable talent and diligence. A fact of note: these practices are particularly harmful to scholars with affective disorders; they threaten neurodiversity. By losing these worlds of talent and experience, universities lose both the expansive imaginations and the sensitivity that people with affective disorders bring. In addition, as universities ponder how to serve what seems to be an increasing number of students with mental illness, they are losing one of the best resources they have to address that problem – successful adults who have lived with these illnesses. Although much attention is given to students in crisis, students who have survived such crises and are struggling to live and work with affective disorders may need even more urgent support. To show these students that writers and teachers with affective disorders can thrive – sometimes in spite of their disorders and occasionally because of them – will give them hope, which is the most important thing we can give.

4
Gaps on the Vita

Sharon O'Brien

Abstract: *"My vita is Swiss cheese", Sharon O'Brien proclaims in this warm, revealing account of a highly accomplished academic writer who must, every year like clockwork, update her curriculum vita to reveal all she has published. Depression, however, can stop productivity in its track; it's downright un-American, at odds with our Franklin-esque devotion to self-reliance and industry, not to mention contemporary ideologies of optimism. Stigma surrounds affective disorders, in particular casting the depressed as malingerers: "If they only tried a little harder, couldn't they just get on with it?" At professional conferences populated by those "hipper and more famous than me", O'Brien's interior monologue rings familiar: "You published a book? I raise you one Ativan. An important, well-reviewed book? I raise you two Ativan." Recovery from depression is complex, but the simplest of acts – like opening Word, or keeping a writing date with a colleague – reveal to O'Brien that she is far from alone.*

Keywords: Affective disorders; academic writers; depression; writing productivity; stigma; curriculum vitae

Horton, Stephanie Stone, ed. *Affective Disorder and the Writing Life: The Melancholic Muse*. Basingstoke: Palgrave Macmillan, 2014. DOI: 10.1057/9781137381668.

Every year, each faculty member at Dickinson College receives an email from the Dean's office requiring us to send in an updated curriculum vita. New entries for work done in the previous year are always at the top of the list, so that the members of the Faculty Personnel Committee can easily see what their colleagues have produced. "Production" in this context means publication. Faculty members are supposed to be productive, which means generating a steady output of published scholarship or creative work, articles, essays, or books arriving like trains, on schedule, on time. When the directive comes to send in the updated CV, it's accompanied by the expectation that there really should have been some publication, some signs of academic life, over the last year.

Earlier in my academic life, I was producing books and articles in a steady stream: two biographies of Willa Cather, a memoir, dozens of articles and chapters in books. I was bold and cocky. Each year, sending in my CV, I put all my new publications and accomplishments into italics so that any bystander could see how productive I had been in the last 12 months. *Look at all those italics! What a dynamo she is!* Now, when the depression I struggle with arrives more frequently – an unwelcome guest – two or three years might go by without a publication. Then I slink through the annual CV request with all my past publications in Roman type; no italics headline recent accomplishments.

When a faculty member has no publications to report for any given year – nothing in italics – what ensues are the dreaded gaps on the vita. What has she been doing with her time, the Dean will wonder. Why is a publication in 2004 followed by one in 2009? Where are the achievements?

It's an odd phrase, "curriculum vitae", as what is recorded on this document is not life but work – the measurable aspect of life that matters to an institution. When someone suffers from a mood disorder, as I do from depression, these gaps on the vita are, in another sense, gaps in the life, hollowed-out, empty spaces when, as William Styron describes depression, one has "slowed-down responses, near paralysis, psychic energy throttled back close to zero" (417). These are times when just going to the store can be a heroic journey, when cleaning a bedroom or washing clothes can be a momentous task. These are times when the mail piles up, creating scary stacks of paper. What is hiding there? Some unknown bill that means the Borough will cut off my water? A tax bill that I will never pay and my house will be repossessed? And what about the crack in the ceiling? It was always there, and I had gotten used to it, but one night the surrounding plaster crashed down on the floor, creating a gaping hole. I managed to sweep up the fallen plaster but the crack was still there, exposing the fragility of the second floor, the fragility of my life. I knew I had to find the energy to hire a contractor to repair the ceiling but meanwhile I tried to ignore this gap, changing my seating so that I could watch television without the visual reminder that my house was crumbling around me.

During these periods of depression, my professional challenge is to meet my classes, hold appointments with my students, return papers in two weeks or less and perform the role of the competent professor. These efforts take all my energy. I've never missed a class, but there is nothing left for writing.

Let me make one thing clear: I think that writing and publication are important parts of the academic life. They keep us connected to the larger world of writers and readers and they enrich our teaching. When I am not able to write, I miss it, even though I cannot do it. But my focus here is not on the reasonable, positive academic expectations for writing and publication; rather, on the expectations for regular, metronomic productivity – visible and frequent signs that publication is taking place. When I cannot perform this productivity, when depression has settled beside me onto the couch while I'm watching *Project Runway* and trying to avoid looking at the crack in my ceiling, I judge myself by the standards I cannot meet. I am ashamed. I do not have any italics to send to the Dean.

* * *

Last year I entered into a long period of depression that has a new companion – worry. Worry tags along after depression, I think, because I'm getting older. "When are you thinking about retiring?" asks a colleague, imagining, I assume, a new tenure line opening up for a younger person. "I'm not thinking about it", I say, privately planning to be the oldest professor ever to teach at my institution. I will be a landmark, a monument to time. I'm afraid of retirement, afraid of all the gaps that will open in my life. Days are filled with hours that can be excruciating to endure when you are in depression, but at least teaching requires you to get up, get dressed, and show up for class. What will happen when there is no such structure? Will I start watching daytime television? Shouting out answers to *Jeopardy?*

It's been easy, until now, to avoid thinking about getting older because I'm the kid sister. My older sister and I have always ascended up the decades together, always eight years apart. She's the one who experiences those scary birthdays first (60! 65!) Being the youngest doesn't mean much anymore. Now, I'm the one getting the mailings from AARP and Medicare; now I'm the one having to have a yearly conference with a financial advisor. Now I'm the one who has got to think about making a will, think about power of attorney, think about dying. I want to be ready to leave quickly and neatly when that happens. When I think about mortality, I think about mess. Who will clean up the house I will have left so abruptly? Who will get rid of the ancient cans of weed killer lurking in the cellar? Who will enter the attic and find homes for the seven empty plastic crates that live there? Who will take my clothes to Goodwill? I have no children and no family members who live close by. Should I hire someone ahead of time? A post-mortem cleaner-outer?

I try not to think about it, but I look around the house and find myself overwhelmed by the many objects to be dispensed with, ranging from the Scrabble set to the dining room table, from my hairbrush to the refrigerator. I think about the permanence of objects, the impermanence of me. The things in my house take on an unsettling life – so many of them will outlast me. The lamp. The sofa. The stove. The frying pan. The mirror. My garden tools will lean against the shed after my death, and the hose will stay in its limp circles in the basement. All of these things will need to be sold, given away, or thrown out by someone who is not me.

When I prepare for my annual consultation with Jackie, my financial advisor, I have to work hard not to have a panic attack. I don't want to think about retirement, I don't want to think about money, but I have to. Jackie is a perky soul, from Nebraska, so she always says something about Willa Cather to me. She loves TIAA, the bonds part of TIAA-CREF, the "safe" part. "Investing in TIAA is like watching paint dry", she says. Her simile is a little off base, but she means that positive stuff is going to happen – just slowly. Meanwhile CREF, the flashier half of the duo, is composed of stocks and tethered to the whims of financial markets. I'm nervous. After our sessions Jackie always tells me that when I retire I'm going to be fine, but I don't believe it. I look at my future self and I don't like what I see: she doesn't have enough money. She will be homeless. She will be bagging groceries at the Giant. She will hate me for having left her in such a fix.

"You're experiencing anxiety", my psychiatrist says. "This can accompany depression."

So that's what this is. Could it possibly be worse than depression? My anxiety deepens and begins to include the present as well as the future. Should I drive to Philadelphia to see a friend this weekend, or will being in a car, with other cars whizzing by me, be too scary? How should I approach teaching a book I've taught dozens of times before? For days at a time it was all I could do to meet my classes and perform being a normal professor. Then I'd come home and devote myself to the only rituals that seemed to help: making tea and microwaving something marketed as a "bed buddy", a sock-like ribbon of cotton filled with pellets that absorb heat. I start to call it my "Warm Thing", WT for short. I'd lie down, put WT over my eyes, sit up occasionally to drink my tea, lie down again, hands on my stomach, counting my breaths. Was WT, my bed buddy, the best I could do right now for a boyfriend? Probably so. I became very attached to WT, my inanimate companion.

I'd make list of modest, insurmountable things to do and give myself a time goal.

1. Take a shower
2. Get dressed
3. Straighten up downstairs
4. Make tea
5. Go outside for ten minutes
6. Grade two papers
7. Microwave WT
8. Do these in any order! Complete by 2 p.m.! Take a Valium. Took Valium 11:15. Should help in about 15 minutes.
9. Took a shower and washed my hair!
10. Lying in bed with WT.
11. Have a short conversation with someone? Maybe go to yoga?
12. Want to be myself again. How to do that?

My journal entries shrivel up into sentence fragments, predicates divorced from subjects, as my life lost the first person singular.

In the midst of this diabolical mix of depression and anxiety, I had to go to the annual conference of my professional organization, the American Studies Association. Mood disorders run by their own rhythms and take their own time, disrupting the time we want to control ourselves. They do not respect the timing of professional conferences. Just the thought of going to the conference was making me more anxious: all those people! And all those younger people (which means just about everyone), now hipper and more famous than me. "I used to be somebody", Jeff Bridges sings in *Crazy Heart*. "Now I am somebody else." That sums it up. I haven't had a major publication since my memoir – *The Family Silver: A Memoir of Depression and Inheritance* – came out in 2004. That's a lifetime ago in my profession. I've done an edition of a Willa Cather novel and published a couple of articles, but in my world that's peanuts. My vita is literally riddled with gaps. My vita is Swiss cheese.

My psychiatrist gave me a prescription for Ativan to take with me to the conference as backup. You tell me that you have published a book? I raise you one Ativan. An important, well-reviewed book? I see that and raise you two Ativan. You want to know what my next project is, what I'm working on now? I will lie, to myself and you, and tell you I will be writing about Willa Cather's afterlife, all the meanings we've made of her since her death. "That's a great project", you'll say. "Thanks", I will say, knowing there's not enough Ativan in all the world to see me through that project. I go to the conference, stick close to my friends, and get through it. I feel momentary triumph: Sharon 1, Mood Disorder 0. I'm only ahead briefly, but that's something.

A few years ago, my psychiatrist changed my DSM diagnosis from "Treatment Resistant Depression" to "Bipolar II". It didn't really matter to me what my mood disorder was called, but since then I've been taking a combination of medications. I take three mood stabilizers, giving me a "ceiling", my psychiatrist says, so that I don't go too high, and a "floor" so that I don't go too low. I don't think I need the ceiling – no highs, except one hypomanic response to Prozac that was enough to shift me into the bipolar category. And as for the medication that's giving me a floor? The floor must be in the sub-basement, because during those periods when the Ativan seems to be working and the anxiety lifts a little, there's enough depression left to weigh me down every single hour of the day.

The mood stabilizers come in different forms: two fat round white pills (Lamictal): two and a half oval skinny pink pills (Mirapex); one dreadful tasting lozenge-like pill that you put under your tongue and let dissolve (Saphris). Then there's the latest antidepressant, Emsam, which comes in a patch you stick to an unobtrusive part of your body for 24 hours. When you take it off, your skin is shiny and your mood unchanged.

These pills are supposed to work together to relieve anxiety and lift depression, but they must be like members of an English Department, unable to get along, squabbling at meetings, and nursing ancient grudges. Lamictal is the old fogey professor who despises literary theory; Mirapex is the creative writer who thinks the literature teachers never give enough respect to the authors; Emsam is the one who never publishes and has too many advisees to make up for it; and Saphris is the just-hired queer studies expert who gets on Lamictal's nerves. These pills are supposed to help, but they're not. I try visualizing my neurotransmitters responding positively to them. "Get with the program", I tell them. "Learn to get along, create a new curriculum." No response. No agreements reached. The endless English Department meeting continues.

During this period my psychiatrist had decided to change my antidepressant from Lexapro (the one who didn't get tenure) to Emsam. Changing an antidepressant is diabolical. You have to gradually decrease the one that isn't working before you can start the new one. You take 20 milligrams for a week, then 15, then 10. That's three weeks. Then you start the new one. Ten milligrams for a week, then 15 for a week, then 20 for a month. Then two weeks at 30, two weeks at 40. And so on. Going off an antidepressant means tapering slowly, and then the process starts all over again with a new one; this can take many weeks. The depression dragged on for months, covering most of two semesters. "Let's divide into groups", I'd say to my classes. Group work is useful and gives shy students a chance to contribute, but it can also be the last refuge of the professor who does not have the mental stamina to run a whole class. There were times when I simply could not bear to have 25 pairs of beady eyes staring at me while I stumbled to find words to put together into sentences. I'd give the small groups an assignment and roam around the edges of the classroom, checking to see that they were really doing the work and not checking their cell phones or making plans for the weekend. "Okay", I'd say after ten minutes, "time to report back in". They'd talk, and I'd try to be animated, making connections among the groups and linking their insights to the themes of the course, all the while thinking only 15 more minutes to go and this class will be over.

During such a period I have always been able to teach. But I am not able to write. And so I am not productive. Being unproductive means not only that I'm not living up to my college's expectations: it also means that I'm not living up to dominant American ideologies. In order to understand the symbolism of productivity, we have to think about the larger culture in which the university is placed, because productivity – what Benjamin Franklin called "visible industry" – is a central American value.

DOI: 10.1057/9781137381668

In her groundbreaking book *Illness as Metaphor*, Susan Sontag defined illness as both the landscape of biological disease and a socially constructed system of meanings. In her exploration of the metaphors used to describe tuberculosis and cancer, she argued that we never undergo an illness in an unmediated way; cultural attitudes, myths, and definitions shape our experience. And so if cancer is described with military metaphors, it becomes easy to refer to a cancer "victim", or to say that someone is "fighting" the illness. Drawing on Sontag in his memoir *At the Will of the Body*, sociologist Arthur Frank makes a useful distinction between "disease" and "illness" that can help us understand American attitudes toward depression. Disease is the supposedly "objective" phenomenon of the malfunctioning body, whereas illness is the subjective experience of "living through the disease", an experience that is shaped by cultural attitudes (13). If we think of illness as the socially constructed definitions that shape the dominant American response to the disease of depression, we can understand more fully why this mood disorder is stigmatized and why a "gap on the vita" caused by an experience of depression can be experienced as a shameful absence.

All mental illnesses in America are marked with stigma, but there is a particular kind of stigma that surrounds depression. People who suffer from depression can be thought, somehow, to be malingerers – if they only tried a little harder, couldn't they just get out of bed and get on with it? Part of the reason for the stigma is the fact that the illness is invisible – there's no blood test for depression, and so it's hard to "prove" that one is suffering from something verifiable and objective. But more important, I think, is the fact that depression is an un-American inactivity, a deviant state in a culture devoted to self-reliance, upward mobility, and the work ethic. The depressed person flagrantly violates cherished American values – work, energy, visible industry. Depression can mean the crumbling of the will, the inability to act, the disappearance of pleasure; these are blows to our dominant ideologies and assumptions about reality. Even though we are now aware of the biochemical sources of depression, those who suffer from the illness can feel that they are somehow at fault. If only they could exert more will power, perhaps depression would lift.

We never experience an illness in a "pure" or absolute sense; we always experience it through the filter of meanings culture attaches to it. And so when people suffering from depression enter what Sontag called the "kingdom of the ill" they cannot help but interpret it, in part, through cultural metaphors and stories they have internalized – stories about individualism, about pulling yourself up by your bootstraps (3). So depression conflicts with what it means to be American.

In fact, in our production-oriented culture, depression is a flat-out insult to the work ethic. Every time I teach Benjamin Franklin's *Autobiography* or Horatio Alger's *Ragged Dick,* both stories of upward mobility and self-transformation, I think "there's no place for depression in these narratives". "Lose no Time", writes Franklin. "Be always employ'd in something useful." Franklin connects such constant industry with the power of the will, which he terms "Resolution". "Resolve to perform what you ought", he counsels. "Perform without fail what you resolve." Try telling that to someone suffering from depression; you will be giving useless advice and enhancing the stigma that surrounds the illness. A few years ago, I published an article on "Women and Depression" in a local magazine and received a phone call from a woman suffering from chronic depression. "How have you managed?" she asked me. "How do you keep your house clean?" "You can't keep your house clean", I said. Franklin would have said Resolve to keep your house clean.

I look at Franklin's schedule for the day – rise at 5:00, work, read, dine, work, supper, conversation, sleep, every hour accounted for, every hour filled, and I think about what my days can be like when I'm depressed. Stay in bed as long as possible. Get up. Go to work. Put all your energy into passing as normal. Come home. Watch TV. Microwave dinner. Watch TV. Wait for the earliest possible bedtime. "When I was depressed and the kids were in school", a woman in a support group once told me, "after everyone left the house I'd get back in bed and spend the day there".

Benjamin Franklin's schedule. Someone with depression getting through the day. These are stories that do not match.

The cultural pressure to tell stories of upward mobility can also shape depression narratives and turn them into recovery stories – the illness equivalent of the Horatio Alger plot. This story is evident even in William Styron's groundbreaking memoir of depression, *Darkness Visible.* Styron dwells for most of the time in darkness, giving us a devastating and brilliant description of entrapment in depression's darkness:

> The pain is unrelenting, and what makes the condition intolerable is the knowledge that no remedy will come – not in a day, an hour, a month or a minute. If there is mild relief, one knows that it is temporary, more pain will follow. It is hopelessness even more than pain that crushes the soul. (62)

Styron's description gives us the "un-American" quality of this prevalent illness. American culture is imbued with what Barbara Ehrenreich calls the "ideology of optimism": the belief in the power of positive thinking and self-improvement. It's the loss of hope and faith in the future being better than the present that marks depression as the dark side of the American dream and makes it such an isolating illness.

Patterning his narrative on the structure of Dante's *Divine Comedy*, Styron shows his own descent into the hell of suicidal despair, his sojourn in the purgatory of the hospital, and his final ascent to the clear air of recovery. Wanting, understandably, to provide hope for the reader, he gives us the ending of depression's lifting: "whoever has been restored to health has almost always been restored to the capacity for serenity and joy, and this may be indemnity enough for having endured the despair beyond despair" (63). Styron's ending is a spiritual version of the American upward mobility narrative. And so if someone suffers from an illness that is chronic, that does not yield to a cure (or even a remission), Styron's memoir may be a silencing story, telling us that it is possible to speak publicly of one's depression only after one has recovered from it.

Of course, it is not just people with mood disorders who have to deal with gaps on the vita. Faculty members who work at academic institutions that require publication may find writing and publishing difficult or impossible for many reasons: they may have young children, they may be going through a divorce, they may have a chronic illness, they may have finished a project and find that a new one does not quickly emerge. They may be halfway through a project and discover that they hate it. There are, of course, the people who do not care about the pressures for regular publication; they have retired from the world of publishing and conferences, accepted their lower raises, and carry on quite happily with their teaching. But many academics do think they should have a constant rhythm of productivity, which is different from the passion they feel for their research and writing. Some people resolve this dilemma by writing pieces they don't care about but know will be published. "I could have cared less about this little essay they wanted", a colleague told me, "but yes, I admit, I wanted to have something on my vita".

Others find themselves feeling guilty when no written project has emerged like clockwork, at an expected time. A friend who teaches at a large state university writes me:

> This very minute I'm full of guilt about having no written product (to continue the industrial language) to put on my merit evaluation this cycle, in spite of a year off. My CV seems to be gaps and spurts – I'm trying to get used to the fact that this is just how I work, but it doesn't fit the institutional model of repeated, regular achievement.

She found the pressure to publish regularly "paralyzing", she said; it was only when she decided that she didn't have to write anything that ideas started to emerge. So she had to trick herself into writing: remove the guilt and expectations to allow writing to flow naturally.

Another colleague protests the pressure of the "vita gap" for a different reason: the pressure to produce publications at a clockwork-like pace means that there is no time for a "fallow period" when someone might simply be reading, absorbing new ideas, and preparing, perhaps, to go in a new research direction. "The fallow period builds the soil, the foundation" for future research publications, she says. But it does not generate publications. We tend to think of the "fallow period" as a phrase we apply to creative people – who are gifted with the time to let ideas and visions emerge. But don't we want creativity from our academic writers as well? What new directions of thought and scholarship might we be closing down because we can have no gaps? What lackluster, useless articles might we be producing, to be read by a handful of readers, because we prefer the title of an article on a vita to no title at all?

Pressures for regular publication at a large research university, where faculty have a reduced teaching load, take a slightly different form than at liberal arts colleges like my own. At Dickinson, an article is a sign of productivity, a book something to be celebrated. It would be possible to have a positive tenure review here if one's form of publication were articles, not books. Not so at a research university: there, books matter, and they should appear at regular intervals. A colleague of mine at Temple University remembers that his first book was followed by 17 years of "booklessness" – years filled with articles leading to a major book. But during this period he was turned down for a study leave because he hadn't "produced anything in a few years!" In the United Kingdom, conditions are even fiercer. The subsidies that the government gives to universities depends solely on the publication of books at regular intervals.

Such pressures for production reflect the ways in which the university over the last 30 years has become more and more corporate. Competing for declining numbers of students, universities and colleges have to "sell" themselves, and they do so through creating a "brand", a signifier that distinguishes them from others on the market. Having a faculty whose work is measured through publication and productivity signifies the intellectual richness of the university, making it a product that can be sold to prospective buyers. The language of the marketplace has entered the language we use to describe jobs: there's the "job market", which has recently become a buyer's market because there are far fewer jobs than applicants. As a result, expectations for publication can be even higher. "I have friends who delay the finishing date of their thesis as long as possible", a young colleague tells me, "so that there will be more time before publication is expected".

The systems of evaluation reflecting regular, methodical publication – which affect all of us, mood-disordered and non-mood-disordered alike – may match with the scholarly rhythms of some people, while being inimical to the rhythms of others. They may be particularly inimical to the rhythms of people with mood disorders because of their relationship to time.

Mood disorders like depression do not respect chronological time; they disrupt time, they create a gap in time which they fill with slow, poisonous fog. When you are in depression, it's all you can do to answer email, and sometimes you'll let the email pile up to frightening levels. 50 messages! 75! When are you going to crack and start answering them with the phrase "Sorry it's taken me so long to get back to you"? The allowable time elapse between someone sending an email and the expected reply has become shorter and shorter. Academics are expected to check email frequently throughout the day, and each message comes accompanied by its time of origin. When you are moving at depression's slowed-down pace you are aware of chronological time rushing past you, trailing a stream of unanswered emails.

Mood disorders – particularly bipolar disorder, but also depression – can be connected in the popular imagination with creativity and sensitivity, with a sped-up sense of time. The person who experiences "highs" that can be managed may, in fact, be able to work quickly and productively, but when the slide into depression occurs, the ability to work and write slows to a crawl – comes to a stop. In "Having It Out with Melancholy", the poet Jane Kenyon, who suffered from bipolar depression, "had it out" with the romantic notion that depression – melancholy – could be a source of creative inspiration. "A piece of burned meat/wears my clothes, speaks/in my voice, dispatches obligations/haltingly, or not at all" (part 7, ll. 1–4). It is only when medication, for a period, lifts her depression ("the pain stops/abruptly") that she is able to "come back/to my desk, books, and chair" (ll. 16–17). Kenyon's description of the broken link between depression and creativity works for the academic as well as for the poet. In depression, one may be able to "dispatch" obligations but not able to write because one is not really inhabiting, fully, "desk, books, and chair". One is not living in the flow of time but is enduring time, living in the slowed-down world of depression, waiting for the illness to lift, waiting for moments of happiness in which time does not matter.

My psychiatrist and I decide that Emsam – which we tried for weeks at the highest dosage – isn't working. So we taper off and start on Wellbutrin, whom I'm imagining as the cheerful head of another department who's taken over chairing English as a favor to the Dean.

One morning, I wake up and things are different. My dreadful self-consciousness of depression is gone ("here is depressed Sharon doing the dishes"). I get out of bed and the person just seems to be me. The air is clear. The depression has lifted and I can do the things that other people seem to do so easily – go to the store, get the car washed, make a dinner that isn't cereal. I am able to sort through the mail, mow the lawn, do the laundry. The first person singulars return to my journal entries and my "to do" lists include items like "call Cary", "remember to get the birthday card", "check on TIAA-CREF". I take WT and put him (for now he is gendered) into the closet with the towels, noting carefully the location, because who knows when I'll need him again? I'm savvy enough to know this is a period of remission, not recovery. I finally call the contractor who comes to fix the crack in the ceiling, putting up drywall so that I'll never have to see it again. I invite friends over for dinner, I go to the movies, I read.

I have returned to my books and chair, but I have not returned to my desk. I am still unable to write. I've been invited to submit an essay on mood disorders, writing, and the academy for a collection: this topic is perfect for me! Why can't I get started? Every day I say "this is the day I'll start the essay", and I keep putting it off. I am feeling better but writing can be lonely work, and so I avoid it. My computer screen looks reproachful; even my journal and pen are ganging up on me. "Come on, Sharon! We're here! Write one sentence, for God's sake!"

I run into Adrienne, my neighbor who's a poet and, for real, the head of Dickinson's English Department.

"It's so terrible!" she says. "I haven't written anything for weeks!"

"I haven't written anything for a year", I say.

"I have people in my office all the time", she says, "expecting me to do things. I take them home with me in my head. This has to stop."

"I don't have anyone in my office", I say, "but I'm totally stuck."

This is just not acceptable, we both agree. We decide to form a two-person writing group and meet every two weeks. We have to bring something to our meeting, no matter how terrible it is.

It's Sunday morning. Adrienne calls to remind me about our writing date at three o'clock. I haven't written a word since we last talked, but I'm not going to go over to her house empty-handed. I go over to the computer, open up Word, and start to write. Every year each faculty member at Dickinson College receives an email from the Dean's office requiring us to send in an updated curriculum vitae.... By 3 p.m., I have four pages. Our writing promise to each other is filling a gap. The time has flown by.

I don't think about whether the essay I'm writing will end up on my vita. I only think about bringing those four pages to Adrienne. The vita doesn't matter: it only matters that I keep bringing her pages until I have finished my essay.

I don't have to do it alone.

Works cited

Bode, Carl, and Horatio Alger, Jr. *Ragged Dick and Struggling Upward*. New York: Penguin Classics, 1985.
Frank, Arthur. *At the Will of the Body: Reflections on Illness*. Buena Vista, VA: Mariner, 2002. Print.
Franklin, Benjamin. *Benjamin Franklin's Autobiography*. Norton Critical Edition. Chaplin, Joyce, ed. New York: W.W. Norton, 2012. Print.
Kenyon, Jane. "Having It Out with Melancholy". *Poets.org*. Academy of American Poets. Web. 17 June 2013.
Sontag, Susan. *Illness as Metaphor and AIDS and Its Metaphors*. New York: Picador, 2001. Print.
Styron, William. *Darkness Visible: A Memoir of Madness*. New York: Modern Library, 2007. Print.

5
Lunatic

Jeannie Parker Beard

Abstract: *Socratic dialectic thrives – it actually rollicks – on the question "Just what is 'crazy', anyway?" The interlocutors include Jeannie, an English professor, and her 43-year-old brother, legally named "Lunatic Michael Culpepper" ("You can't make this stuff up", Jeannie posits). Lunatic's bipolar illness fuels his unconventional and prolific writing life, and has since the Internet opened innumerable avenues for his myriad interests. His posts, including 17,000-plus tweets, have attracted some 2,000 followers; in coded languages, he explores madness, Hermeticism, quantum physics, the Gnostics (or "Ga-nostics"), and much more. Lunatic serves as muse to his sister's writing, and his dialectical musings on magic offer a clear sense of the real:*

JEANNIE: *"So what is magic? Tell me the opposite of magic."*
LUNATIC: *"Having no power."*
JEANNIE: *"Wow. That's pretty good. That's why rhetoric was considered a form of magic."*
LUNATIC: *"Because it is powerful."*

Keywords: Madness; dialectic; bipolar disorder; the writing life

Horton, Stephanie Stone, ed. *Affective Disorder and the Writing Life: The Melancholic Muse.* Basingstoke: Palgrave Macmillan, 2014. DOI: 10.1057/9781137381668.

What I'm about to tell you is absolutely true; it illustrates that truth is often stranger, and more interesting, than fiction, and the dialectic method is still applicable to real-world situations in the present day.

My brother, who is 12 years my senior, is bipolar. He's been self-medicating for years, which means he has done just about every street drug imaginable, except ones involving needles. He's too squeamish and cleanly for needles. About six years ago, he went through a speed kick. He was also taking fat burners – which, from my understanding, can literally destroy the fat lining around the nerves, giving a new and painfully more accurate meaning to the term "nervous breakdown". We really noticed something was wrong when, in his mania, he climbed up a tree in my parents' front yard and cut half of it down, all the while screaming, *"I'm Jesus Christ! I'm Jesus Christ! I live forever!"* Of course, my parents wanted the limbs trimmed, but they didn't expect it to go down quite like that.

During this time, my brother was in a full-fledged stage of mania, and he was wild. I wish I had time to go into the details, but the short of it is that he was always up to some mischief, which usually involved staying up for days, chanting at his makeshift altar, burning incense, and lining the walls of his apartment with symbols and pictures cut out of his extensive collection of esoteric books. He has been in trouble with the law for the most mundane things: theft by taking when he stole a rosary from a Catholic church (the nun was just scared of him, so she called the cops); terrorist threats (he told a man who was making advances on his wife, Janet, that he was "hired by Janet's husband to kill" him (the guy didn't realize that he was Janet's husband); and for displaying his back full of tattoos to the kids on a playground at a local daycare – basically, all harmless things that only a person experiencing the heights of mania would do. He is full of energy, so much so that he overwhelms people. I am confident that if he were to step into a room that was equipped with sensitive instruments that measure energy frequencies, he would send the meters off the charts, and probably blow some fuses. He is also the smartest and most insightful person I know without a formal education.

My brother never went to college, but he has always been a voracious reader. It's the things that he reads that are questionable to some people. He is really into Hermetics, alchemy, ancient philosophy, world religions (Western and Eastern), the Gnostics (he pronounces it "Ga-nostics"), the Freemasons, the Illuminati, quantum physics, and the occult. He has tattoos of ancient symbols all over his body, along with a wizard and dragon, and various Chinese characters. He is intensely enamored with symbolism. He believes in magic. And when he's off his medicine, the "ghosts" tell him things. Honestly, he reminds me of a modern-day William Blake, and like Blake in his own day, my brother is sadly misunderstood. I'm one of the few people who really understand him – me and Janet, his wife of nearly 20 years. I see the wisdom and genius that shines through his hysteria and mania.

Five years ago, in the midst of an intense and ongoing period of mania, my brother decided to legally rename himself "Lunatic". He went to the judge, was denied, and then went back with the defense that it was his Constitutional right to change his name to anything he wanted. The judge, disgruntled and bewildered, signed the paper, and my brother's name is now officially "Lunatic Alan Michael Culpepper". (Seriously, my brother's name is Lunatic. You can't make this stuff up.) He loves to flash his driver's license at any opportunity. He gets junk mail addressed to "Lunatic Culpepper". When he goes to the doctor, they call him "Mr. Lunatic". It gives him quite a thrill.

Lunatic has reasons for choosing this name. He says it's mystical. He also claims that he can never be prosecuted under the law because in the legal dictionary it states that lunatics cannot be tried. I don't know if this is necessarily true, but he somehow manages to get out of any trouble he gets into. Most recently, in a mania, he was standing on the side of the road at a busy intersection jumping up and down screaming, "I'm crazy! I'm crazy! I'm the Lunatic!" The cop (invariably a cop is going to show up in a scenario such as this) simply called my parents and had them come pick him up and drive his car home so he didn't have to drive (my brother is 43 years old, and the police call his parents when he misbehaves). Lunatic said he and the officer had a nice conversation while they were waiting. The ghosts make him do some strange things, but he's totally harmless, and really, he is exceptionally sweet. He's actually one of my favorite people in the world. I'd much prefer him to some of my "normal" relatives. For one, he's more interesting, but more importantly, he has this in-depth, perceptive (however skewed) view of reality that makes me believe in the potential for highly evolved consciousness within the human race. And that makes me hopeful.

Lunatic has been on his medication and out of trouble for a while now. When he's on his meds, he seems relatively normal, but there are still many things that are undeniably special about him. He manages to fly right under the radar when he stays on his medicine.

Though a voracious reader, Lunatic always had an aversion to writing and never did well in school. He had problems with language, saying words correctly, and knowing how to spell correctly, and he has trouble communicating his feelings without overwhelming people. He is so self-conscious about his writing that for years he has had his wife write birthday cards from him because of his dyslexia. Though never tested, he would probably be labeled with a number of learning disabilities. For years, my brother never wrote, and would have never considered himself a writer.

But the Internet and social media have changed all that. Lunatic has become a prolific user of social media in recent years; now, he identifies himself as a writer as he Tweets every day, sometimes hundreds of times, and is also a very active contributor on many social network platforms. My brother's mastery of social media baffles me, really, as he has taught himself how to do anything and everything related to these sites (and self-promotion on them), yet he has no formal education or training whatsoever. He actually teaches me things about how to use social media sites on a regular basis, and he is dialed into all the latest trends.

My brother writes in his own coded language, using wordplay and mystical configurations of letters, sounds, and symbols. His posts demonstrate a clever compensation for lack of spelling ability through his crafty changing of the words to have not only different spellings but also double meanings:

JOIN IN ... AS

AH=BOVE<)))))SOUL==BEE/LOW ... AS ... WITH=()IN ... SOUL=O ... B.E

What is so fascinating about Lunatic's writing is that he uses word and letter play not only to write often complex coded language, but also to overcome the sense of shame and insecurity that he felt for most of his life when it came to literacy and his ability to communicate through the written word.

Part of his inspiration for changing the spelling of words and creating double meanings also comes from his study of Hermeticism, a school of thought that includes a deep interest in etymology and how words have hidden (magical) meanings – for example, Adam (the first man) relates to atom; Lunatic might construct this as KNOW-1-EDGE, and a myriad of connections of that nature. Also, Lunatic informs me that the study of Kabbalah deals with the composition of words, their codes and relationships, and the magical influence of language in the creation of reality. The study of these concepts is actually pretty in depth, and though Lunatic's writing is on the surface psychotic, it is also extensive, and without a doubt, there is brilliance to it.

Here is another example of a Tweet that includes a world of depth and play that many might miss:

> "CLASS A:A NEW Aeon ... IS/IS==HERE ... KNOW UR OCCULT LOGO'SS ... 4 THE [PORT]A.L ... ((((IS)))o)PAN ..."

In this short, cryptic message, Lunatic refers to a new eon (the Age of Aquarius); Isis, the Egyptian goddess; the symbolic nature of logos; Secret Societies (SS); binary code (represented by the zero); and Pan, the pagan god of the wild. I am probably missing a few things, but knowing him and his interests, I can easily pick up on those references at first glance. Most of the time he addresses his "CLASS", or the people who follow him; he has built up quite a fan base on various sites. Many times he also will say that he is revealing a "CLUE" in his codes, for example, "WHAT DOSE IT TAKE CLUE 2 MAKE A:A GOLD(EN)AGE".

It takes Lunatic no time to come up with his codes. They simply roll off his fingertips. I can usually read them easily, but it takes some practice to be able to automatically decipher the meaning in his musings.

So the man named Lunatic, my brother, is a writer, the most unlikely one imaginable. No one in my family would consider him thus, and most do not even know about this role he plays, but he is a dedicated writer as he writes every day and encourages me to do so as well. Today, Lunatic considers himself a real writer; he defines a "real writer" as "someone who writes every day". As I've progressed through several degree programs, he has always supported me with this advice – to simply BE a writer by writing every day. And now he is leading by example – the very last person I would have ever imagined to be a model and inspiration for my own writing habits.

There are pages and pages of Lunatic code on his Twitter and Facebook feeds. He has over 2,000 followers, people interested in similar subjects and ideas, and many people who understand and "like" his daily musings. To date, he has written 17,126 Tweets, and that number climbs with each passing day. His messages convey a profundity and absurdity of sorts, revealing mysteries about the essence of life, spiritualism, the nature of the universe, as well as the very nature of words, language, and the power of letters to communicate thoughts, even when they are not composed in a way that we have been taught to recognize.

My brother's life reveals a story about creating, connecting, and psychosis, the symbolism of words and letters, and ultimately the meditative, curative power of writing and the state of BE-I-NG a writer, as he might put it.

Lunatic, Janet, and I like to take walks when I visit my parents. We walk around the streets of downtown Kennesaw and philosophize about things, I imagine much like Socrates and his companions did so long ago. It's interesting – the Lunatic and the English professor, hashing things out on an evening stroll. The following is an actual conversation we recently had on one of our walks. It started out simple enough, but I realized immediately that it had the potential to be an exercise in the dialectical method, so I attempted to guide it as such. This is, roughly, how it went. By the way, Lunatic calls me Bean.

It is a brisk evening in November, an hour before dusk. We are strolling past the familiar houses in the neighborhood where we grew up. Lunatic looks pensive. He's been in a good mood all day, and has been feeling generally good lately. I'm excited and stressed, happy and anxious about the many things going on in my life. Janet is her usual upbeat and cheery self.

LUNATIC: Bean, do you think I'm crazy?
JEANNIE: What?! That's all you've been telling everyone for years! You don't wanna be crazy now?
LUNATIC: I'm just askin', Bean, do you really think I'm crazy?
JEANNIE: Well, yeah. But there is good crazy and bad crazy. Define crazy.
LUNATIC: I don't know. What is crazy?
JANET: Crazy can be a lot of things.
JEANNIE: Yeah. People use crazy in so many different ways. It's not like it's always maniacal, psycho crazy.
LUNATIC: So, what's maniacal?
JEANNIE: No, we can't define that yet. We've got to define crazy first.
LUNATIC: Okay, okay. Then what's crazy, Bean?
JEANNIE: Just think about it, people use crazy for a lot of things. Like sometimes people are the life of the party when they get sauced up and act all crazy. People will say, "I love her! She's so crazy!"
JANET: Yeah, is that why all your friends like to get you drunk?
JEANNIE: (Laughing) Nah, it's because of my awesome singing and break dancing. But seriously, we have to define crazy. A common definition of crazy is when somebody does the same thing over and over and expects different results.
JANET: In that case, yes, Lunatic, you're crazy.

LUNATIC: How you figure?
JEANNIE: You have all kinds of rituals and things that you do. You wear that hat (it is custom made, and it says RAB EYE on the front, and some other symbolic numbers that give a message I can't remember), and that necklace, and you carry around all that stuff in your pocket – a feather, an ounce of silver and gold, incense, crystals – expecting different results.
LUNATIC: I'm not expecting different results. I'm just doing magic.
JANET: Okay, what's magic then?
JEANNIE: I'm not satisfied with the definition of crazy yet. We need to come up with one of our own. I'm pretty sure there's more to crazy than just doing the same thing over and over. What is the opposite of crazy? We can get our definition if we know what it's not.
JANET: The opposite of crazy is ordinary.
JEANNIE: Okay, that's good. So crazy is out of the ordinary.
JANET: Yes, because according to the legal system, someone is crazy if they are doing things that are out of the ordinary. I know 'cause that's what they told us in court.
LUNATIC: So we're talking about the herd mentality here. The collective group determines what's normal, and they are the ordinary.
JANET: So we will define ordinary as what is everyday behavior and activity, as defined by the masses, and crazy as out of the ordinary.
JEANNIE: Yeah. I'll go with that definition because it can apply to the many different types of crazy there are. So, if crazy is out of the ordinary, I would say you are crazy, Lunatic.
JANET: Well, isn't everyone crazy in some ways?
JEANNIE: By our definition, that can't be, because if everyone was crazy, it would be ordinary to be crazy.
JANET: Yeah, that makes sense.
JEANNIE: If you think about it, crazy is really subjective. It all depends on what context you are in. Some people believe the crazy things Lunatic believes.
JANET: What makes him crazy though is that he believes all of it. He believes in all the religions and all those different ideologies. People might believe in one of his ideas, but they don't believe in ALL of it like he does.
LUNATIC (WILDLY LAUGHING): Yeah, I believe it all! Hermetics, Gnostics ("Ga-nostics"), ancient symbols, witchcraft. I've got it all covered! He starts to lift his shirt to show his tattoos, something he does often.
JANET: Yeah, yeah, put your shirt down. We've seen them all before. See, that's what makes you out of the ordinary.
JEANNIE: Yes, but all that stuff is really underlying the myths of all religions. So, no, I don't think his beliefs are really what make him crazy. It's his actions. It's how he acts that makes him seem crazy to ordinary people around here. People living in the bush of Africa do rituals and have customs that we think

are crazy, but they are normal to them, and they're not considered crazy. If they come here and do their rituals, we would think they were crazy.

JANET: It's all cultural. Beliefs are a cultural thing. So when you believe something that is not common in your culture, it seems crazy. Like those Heaven's Gate people, or when the Mormon church got started. A belief has to become part of the culture for people to accept it as not crazy. What you do (to Lunatic) when you act out is crazy.

LUNATIC: So it's crazy for me to believe in magic?

JEANNIE: What's magic? No, tell me the opposite of magic.

LUNATIC: Having no power.

JEANNIE: Wow. That's pretty good. That's why rhetoric was considered a form of magic.

LUNATIC: Because it's powerful.

JANET: I call it manipulation. No, actually, I call it persuasion.

JEANNIE: Well, that's what it is. And it is powerful.

LUNATIC: Yeah, just look at the mass programming you see everywhere. All the programming, all the marketing, all the people doing their part to fit in the hive, the hundredth monkey effect.

JEANNIE: If you think about it, religious people believe in magic. Your kind of magic just isn't popular, although I still say other people think the way you do. You just haven't met them before.

LUNATIC: So to be crazy, you have to be deranged, incompetent, crazed?

JEANNIE: Crazed, maybe, but not necessarily deranged or incompetent. You just have to appear out of the norm.

LUNATIC: So just walking down the street, you can't just look at me and tell I'm crazy.

JEANNIE: I guess that would be the true test. We could stick you in a picture with one hundred other "ordinary" people, and see if someone could pick you out, the crazy person, the Lunatic.

JANET: Yes, they totally could.

JEANNIE: I agree. You'd have to just show up for the picture dressed like you always dress, and do what you always do for pictures (Lunatic always does something special when he's having his picture made, which he is reluctant to do because it "steals his energy").

LUNATIC, GRINNING: Yeah, you're right. With my magical hat and necklace and all, I probably do stand out.

JEANNIE: So that's what I'll do. I'll take your picture, and compare it to other "normal" people's picture. If you stand out as out of the ordinary, then you're crazy.

We round the corner that leads to my parents' driveway. We've come full circle in our journey.

LUNATIC: One more thing, Bean. I don't really think I'm crazy, because a crazy person wouldn't be able to talk about being crazy.
JEANNIE: Oh yeah, that's another thing people always say! Crazy people don't know they're crazy! So you just denied that you're crazy! That proves you are again!
LUNATIC: Yep. I guess it does.

Part II
"Their Lives a Storm Whereon They Ride": Affective (Dis)order and the Literary Imagination

6
Axing the Frozen Sea: Female Inscriptions of Madness

Joann K. Deiudicibus

Abstract: *"Madness is a solitary malady – and so is writing", offers Joann Deiudicibus in this study of the stark isolation at the heart of depression and the unimaginable pain of various psychic states. At mid-century, Anne Sexton's highs and her suffering, transformed into art, deepened our understanding of madness, poetics, gender, writing-as-therapy, and even conceptions of psychopharmacology and the artist. Contemporary writers describe depression's flipside – the intense heightening and sharpening of the senses often characteristic of mania, and how states of hypomania and mania can escalate creative productivity. Separated from romanticized and gender stereotypes, depression – with its inexorable pull toward death – can be viewed not only in terms of loss, but as creation, composition, and close contemplation of "the gift close to the wound".*

Keywords: Madness; isolation; depression; hypomania; mania; creativity; Anne Sexton

Horton, Stephanie Stone, ed. *Affective Disorder and the Writing Life: The Melancholic Muse.* Basingstoke: Palgrave Macmillan, 2014. DOI: 10.1057/9781137381668.

The books we need are the kind that act upon us like a misfortune, that make us suffer like the death of someone we love more than ourselves, that make us feel as though we were on the verge of suicide, or lost in a forest remote from all human habitation – a book should serve as the ax for the frozen sea within us. (Kafka, qtd. in Kumin 48)

Tell it true

Across the street from our old, red brick apartment building was a tan brick library where I used to go when it was hot before we had air conditioning. I would sit in that library and read poetry or books about serial killers, because I had a morbid mind and liked analyzing words and people. Sometimes I would pretend to read and I would watch the people in the library, instead. The summer I turned 17, even though we had air conditioning by then, I went to the library and walked just around the desk to the poetry section where I picked up some Emily Dickinson. But I wanted something new, so I scanned the shelves until I saw the title: *Live or Die*. I could not move my eyes from the plain, off-white spine with these three commanding words in faded gold lettering. This is where I met Anne Sexton.

Sexton, a Modern American confessionalist, soon became my favorite poet. Yet it was not until much later, after I had written about her in graduate school that I began to realize why her words stayed with me, why her focus on gender roles, motherhood, and psychiatric illness resonated with me and still do. (I have never been married, have never had children, and have no such debilitating diagnosis, though now, in my mid-30s, I have known many women who have.) Sexton's courage – to question her predetermined place in the home as solely a wife and mother and to examine the origin of her often-debilitating psychoses – has caused me to defend her momentous work. I relate most of all to the woman–writer who needed words, whose work gave her purpose, who would cultivate an indelible voice that came to represent others quietly grappling with taboo subjects. Sexton's writing abetted other authors to speak about personal trauma; her poems still speak, influencing readers and contemporary female authors today. Ironically, the very conditions that led her to write – the source and primary subject matter that fueled her creativity – also destroyed her.

Sexton undertook regular therapy in 1956 for post-partum depression. Her primary therapist of eight years, Dr Martin Orne, believed instead that she was suffering from hysteria and recurring depressions, which taxed her memory. At Orne's suggestion, she began writing poetry as a way to remember, to reflect, and to build self-esteem. "Once Anne was assured that she really was able to write poetry, she almost could not stop", notes her biographer, Diane Wood Middlebrook (xiv). Sexton admitted later that she continued to write mainly because of Orne's encouragement (42).

After a suicide attempt in 1957, Dr Orne said, "You can't kill yourself, you have something to give. Why, if people read your poems (they were all about how sick [she] was) they would think, 'There's somebody else like me!' They wouldn't feel alone ..." [Sexton remarked,] "I had found something to do with my life" (43). From her psychoses and skill grew an impressive oeuvre that would bring her fame in her own lifetime. Ultimately, her publications helped numerous readers who often wrote to her in search of affirmation. Her daughter, Linda, recalls, "My mother always said, 'Tell it true', and I believe she thought, as I do, that it is important to share the experience of depression with others, who may be suffering in the same way" ("A Tortured Inheritance").

Writing allowed Sexton to become an active patient in her therapy. She would listen to recordings of and take notes on her sessions to identify key themes and consider her emotions (Middlebrook xv–xvi). In words, she found her calling, a home. Writing was not a cure-all, but it certainly prolonged her life. However, according to Middlebrook:

> The period of Sexton's therapy (1956–1974) coincided with vast, ongoing changes in the understanding of mental illness.... The use of "hysteric" as a diagnostic term applied almost exclusively to women, for example, it was discarded as the name for a clinical disorder during Sexton's lifetime.... Researchers in the field of biologically based psychiatric problems have proposed that current diagnostic methods might have revealed a manic-depressive illness at the base of Sexton's disturbances. (403)

If Sexton were born later, her illness might have been properly diagnosed and treated, extending her life; whether her writing would have remained the same is another matter.

The fool's disease

> In this place everyone talks to his own mouth.
> That's what it means to be crazy.
> Those I loved best died of it –
> the fool's disease. (ll. 245–248)
> Anne Sexton, "Flee on Your Donkey" – June 1962

DOI: 10.1057/9781137381668

The connections between affective disorders and creativity, particularly the relationship between moods, muse, and the writing process, have been well explored by authors, therapists, and scholars. The extensive research of Dr Kay Redfield Jamison, Professor of Psychiatry, has significantly altered notions of the exchange between creativity and mental illness. From the personal to the clinical, Jamison explores the nuanced complexities and dynamics of the subject. *An Unquiet Mind: A Memoir of Moods and Madness* offers her story of being diagnosed with and managing bipolar disorder, elucidating much about this often misunderstood and misdiagnosed condition. In fact, "The major clinical problem in treating [patients with] manic–depressive illness is... [that due to] a lack of information, poor medical advice, stigma, or fear of personal and professional reprisals, they do not seek treatment at all" (Jamison 6).

Sexton and other writers, including her daughter Linda Gray Sexton (*Half in Love: Surviving the Legacy of Suicide*), Jamison (*An Unquiet Mind; Touched with Fire: Manic–Depressive Illness and the Artistic Temperament*), and Marya Hornbacher (*Madness: A Bipolar Life*) have dragged the dark topic of madness into day, illuminating the toil of surviving its tempestuous emotions and related suicide attempts through body motif and disturbing, often grotesque imagery. These women share a compulsion to create, to harness words as an exploration of mood and self. Their writings demystify madness, exposing the intricacy of living with, recovering from, and preventing psychological breakdowns. The act of telling dispels shame surrounding the subject, offering threads of hope to readers.

Anne Sexton's first book, *To Bedlam and Part Way Back*, selectively details her journey through initial psychological breakdowns and her near return to sanity. As James Dickey comments, this collection gathers the feelings "of madness and near-madness, of the pathetic, well-meaning, necessarily tentative and perilous attempts at cure, and of the patient's slow coming back into the human associations and responsibilities which the old, previous self still demands" (63). Reintegrating into one's former life after institutionalization is crushing, as these writers present, and there are few available models to ease the transition. Perhaps the speaker/patient/author cannot fully return or recover, as images of asylum haunt her always. These writers characterize institutionalized patients as children or invalids to convey the incapacitation and dependency that prevents them from functioning in society.

Bedlam's introductory poem "You, Doctor Martin", directly addresses Dr Martin Orne, who nonchalantly "[walks]/from breakfast to madness" (ll. 1–2). Sexton creates a ghastly image of patients: "the moving dead still talk/of pushing their bones against the thrust/of cure" (ll. 4–6). They thrash against leather and metal restraints, "pushing" as the body involuntarily convulses during shock therapy, or "pushing" toward wellness desperately. The multivalent image depicts the hellishness of healing. The sexual connotation of "thrust", that vigorous yet violent action juxtaposed with the stark white bones of the "moving dead" is striking. There is no fecundity, only the body going through the uncontrollable motions. The speaker explains, "We chew in rows, our plates/scratch and whine like chalk/in school" (ll. 13–15), evoking their powerlessness within madness, which reduces them to a humiliating physical and psychological place; patients must concede to the authority of the doctors who enforce strict schedules of pointless tasks and dehumanizing treatments. She continues, "What large children we are/here" (ll. 29–30). Sexton's enjambment of "here" emphasizes that the patients do not fulfill the dependent role of "children" consistently when they are not in asylum. Madness also becomes another misunderstood thing, like the captives who ramble, their words ignored or deemed incomprehensible: "And we are magic talking to itself,/noisy and alone.../... Am I still lost?" (ll. 37–39). Her final, unanswered question contrasts the penultimate line's clamor, echoing the loneliness of madness.

In *Bedlam*'s "Music Swims Back to Me", another lost, mad speaker addresses a stranger: "Wait Mister. Which way is home?" (ll. 1–2). The poem's disorienting language mimics how the patient feels trapped within disordered senses and in this place for the mentally unsound. "Four ladies over eighty,/in diapers every one of them" (ll. 5–6) present the invalid motif, extending the loss of control over not only the mind but also the debilitated body. The speaker continues, "[I]...danced in a circle" (l. 13), ironically free although the image also implies habits of insanity; she follows one pattern obsessively, returning to the beginning that melds into the end. Such are the cycles of madness. Sexton's personification creates transference of agency to music whose structure and familiar refrain appeal to the chaotic mind. The duality of music reflects the duality of insanity. Those deemed insane are confined by stigma, but the label is simultaneously liberating. The mad have no decorum.

Sexton's sharp imagery affronts our senses: "strangled cold", "stars strapped in the sky", and "the moon ... too bright" (ll. 19–21): the inhospitable temperature; the once wishful symbols restrained against the night's vast nothingness; and the glaring moon summoning lunatics who have "a singing in the head" (l. 23). The speaker concludes this stanza: "I have forgotten all the rest" (l. 24) including her way home, to sanity. Finally, we complete the circle as we meet again at the first word of the poem: "Mister", once an address, now an interrogation. The speaker remains directionless, stuck in this place of madness where she began.

Sexton shows madness fully, not simply as a romanticized or devilish stereotype. She unlocks the asylum doors to reveal patients with "the fool's disease", demoralized by demeaning treatment that excises autonomy (248). Similarly, in *Half in Love*, Linda Sexton conveys terror at her indeterminate stay in the psychiatric ward: "The idea that I was somewhere that had no exit terrified me…. [A]n old woman passed by me with her soiled nightgown…. 'They're talking to me again. The wolf is the loudest'" (*Half* 125–126). The invalid motif threatens with the possibility of abandonment, of becoming too sick to return to one's former life. A patient's impaired judgment results in dependency on the sane; Linda recalls, "How strange it was to feel like a child again, under supervision, as I painted and played with crayons…. so sad and ineffectual; here I was doing more of my mother's gig" (144). She has regressed like the figures in her mother's poems, and like her mother did. Similarly, Marya Hornbacher writes of her second husband: "No one should have to be up for this. He signed on for a marriage, not for taking care of an invalid wife", illustrating her guilt for the myriad demands of her illness (202). The fear and fallacies surrounding affective disorders wear on these women, as well as on their spouses, relatives, and friends. As Jamison reminds us, bipolar disorder is "an illness … that brings in its wake almost unendurable suffering and, not infrequently, suicide" (*Unquiet Mind* 6). A person with bipolar disorder typically takes an estimated ten years to seek treatment (Hornbacher 282); thus, securing a proper diagnosis and a successful treatment plan is also a time-consuming investment with many false starts. Furthermore, a person with a serious psychiatric disorder has a reduced life span of 25 years compared to a person without one (281). These images and facts are bleak, but they shock us into reevaluating our presumptions of mental illness, and call us to act with a newfound empathy for its residents.

Milking the unconscious

In language, Anne Sexton controlled compulsively on paper what surged under the thin armor of her skin. In "The Black Art", she admits: "A woman who writes feels too much,/those trances and portents" (ll. 1–2). She, like many writers with affective disorders, could readily break the surface of the frozen sea and access the turbulent current of a telling unconscious below. In a 1968 interview by Barbara Kevles, Sexton reveals, "Sometimes my doctors tell me that I understand something in a poem that I haven't integrated into my life. In fact, I may be concealing it from myself, while I was revealing it to the readers. The poetry is often more advanced, in terms of my unconscious, than I am. Poetry, after all, milks the unconscious" (McClatchy 5). Orne's decision to release Sexton's therapy tapes posthumously to her biographer remains controversial as it broke doctor–patient confidentiality. He did believe that Sexton would have wanted to help others in sharing her story. Middlebrook reiterates, "I don't think Anne Sexton cared what was known about her private life", she said. "She just didn't want to be known as a bad artist" (402). Her daughter and literary executor, Linda, agreed.

Anne Sexton believed, "The only source of greatness was the writer's ability 'to go down deep' into the unconscious.... [I]t doesn't matter how you get there, but it has to dive down. That's what I try to do in a poem, though I don't always succeed" (Middlebrook 165). She admits to failure but remarks that the journey and process of self-discovery, or simply the discovery of an image or phrase, is key.

These mined bits do not always become a finished, engaging, cohesive poem, but they might become the start of another poem, or the core image of a prose passage, or spark an association for a title. This is true of my own writing, as well. Often I'll begin to write and cannot tell the worth or meaning of what comes. I don't always realize until later when I am rearranging images or fragments that they symbolize my own thorny, recurring concerns: my body's aberrant immune responses, my long-term relationship with abandonment, and my conflict regarding my reunion with my biological mother. Writing is an itch under the skin where I begin to scratch, widening the microscopic tear. Poems live there.

Regarding E.H. Gombrich's idea that "the theory of art as a form of self expression... is a relatively modern one", researchers from Emory College conclude, "writing is not always an exercise of conscious cognition"

DOI: 10.1057/9781137381668

(Thomas and Duke 216). Similarly, Bolton distinguishes between prose writers and poets regarding the source of their work:

> [I]t appears that...poets...dealt with the unconscious first, and still deal with it more predominantly. Writing poetry is like psychoanalysis; both take the patient/writer to previously unexplored areas of their consciousness. The earliest phases of individual composition tend to be driven by instinct and tend to lack reasoning. (qtd. in Thomas and Duke 216)

This is true of brainstorms and drafts, yet the process of organizing, revising, and editing compulsively until the work is refined fosters feelings of lucidity and stability for many writers. Sexton remarks, "... [W]riting actually puts things back in place. I mean, things are more chaotic, and if I can write a poem, I come into order again, and the world is again a little more sensible, and real. I'm more in touch with things" (Colburn 72). Writing performs a similar function for me. Something I may not have considered cogently yet might spring forth; after a few drafts, the poem is telling me where it needs to go. Whether the work is autobiographical, or merely a subconscious image or phrase that suddenly repeats in my mind, it is of me and represents me in how I compose it ultimately, if not in its content. Having control over textual arrangement, diction, and figurative language is empowering. Writing connects me to a still somehow familiar place within I do not fully at first seem to remember; it connects me to others who have written about the same topics, or who then read what I have written.

As J.D. McClatchy asserts in his preface to *Anne Sexton: The Artist and Her Critics*: "... [H]er revelations are always forceful because of their intimacy, and valuable because of their authenticity. And their effect is always purposive: to create shocks of recognition in her reader" (vii). Sexton's popularity is testimony to the magnitude of those shocks: "The peculiar power of the lyric poem has always been its ability to enlist a reader's empathetic identification; Sexton understood this very well, and it helped focus her as an artist" (Middlebrook 273).

When asked why she does not write many joyful poems, Sexton explains to Barbara Kevles: "Pain engraves a deeper memory" (Colburn 108). Katherine M. Thomas and Marshall Duke pose the question: "Do authors suffering from depression write differently than psychologically healthy ones?" (205). Citing a 2004 study of the writing of nine suicide poets compared with nine non-suicide poets, they determine that those "who committed suicide used more first person words (I, me, my, and so forth) than poets who never attempted suicide" (205). Results were the same in the writing of depressed versus non-depressed college students. Hence, Thomas and Duke propose that textual analysis could detect depression in authors of both poetry and prose (205). They define depression as per David Wedding's analysis of Sexton's poems, which exhibit multiple cognitive distortions common to thought patterns of suicides: arbitrary inference, selective abstraction, overgeneralization, magnification or hyperbole, minimization, personalization, and dichotomous thinking (206–208). Notably, the period of 1940–1960 had the "highest rate of cognitive distortions... because of [its] many confessional poets" (216). Even so, Sexton concedes that illness alone does not guarantee authorial success: "I don't think genius and insanity grow in the same bed, I think the artist must have a heightened awareness. It is seldom this sprouts from mental illness alone" (Colburn 71). Skilled artists must learn to be receptive; cultivating this awareness resuscitates muse.

Sexton's choice of Kafka's dictum as the preface to the collection *To Bedlam and Part Way Back* is all too appropriate, illustrating her desire to confront the underbelly of contentment's veneer. She wanted to submerge herself in the experience of what she read and, in turn, to recreate the intensity of her suffering ("on the verge of suicide, or lost... remote from all human habitation") in writing for others. About her own poetry as "the ax for the frozen sea" (Kafka qtd. in Kumin 48), she comments: "Absolutely. I feel it should do that. I think it should be a shock to the senses. It should almost hurt" (Colburn 72). Erica Jong refers to this as "skinlessness" in her article "Remembering Anne Sexton": "the gift [of language] is useless without the curse:... eyes that see so sharply they often want to close" (2). Nevertheless, for years Sexton's eyes did not close because she wrote, and because, as she said, "Suicide is, after all, the opposite of the poem" (Sexton and Ames 273). Writing provided a sense of confidence and immortality. As Sexton explains to Dr Orne: "I've taken care of the 'live' part by writing my poems... I've hung on all those times! That was going to be the reason I lived, anyway" (Middlebrook 165).

The gender of things

That day in the library when I picked up Sexton's *Live or Die*, I skimmed the table of contents engaged by the poem: "Wanting to Die". (Who could ignore a title like that?) Encapsulating her morbid fascinations and defending her *thanatos*, this poem stuck to me that day in the library – its visceral imagery and troubling topic. One of the best examples of Sexton's attitude toward her suicidal impulses lives in the poem "Wanting to Die", written on 3 February 1964. Published in 1966, *Live or Die* named the question she struggled with every day.

Although writing was crucial in sustaining Sexton's life, it was only a temporary solution. In the article, "Why Doesn't the Writing Cure Help Poets?" James Kaufman and Jenal Sexton observe,

> Women having a heightened awareness of extrinsic constraints could lead to increased mental stress for female writers. As a writer gains critical and public acclaim, the extrinsic constraints – such as reviews, attention, royalties, and evaluations, become more and more salient.... Producing a highly creative work under extrinsic constraints is more difficult than doing so under intrinsic motivation conditions. (Amabile 273)

Kaufman and Sexton suggest that women are not readily able to dismiss external pressures in the way that men are, as women seek validation explicitly. This may apply to Sexton, whose literary career rapidly reached celebrity status. Once publishing deadlines and readings (the latter caused her severe anxiety) became part of her routine, so did the demands to produce more and better work. Although Sexton's second collection *All My Pretty Ones* (1962) was well received, certainly not all the critics were encouraging. In the *New York Times* review on 28 April 1963, James Dickey was ruthless: "It would be hard to find a writer who dwells more insistently on the pathetic and disgusting aspects of bodily experience, as though this made the writing more real ..." (Sexton and Ames 166). Sexton later commented to a fellow poet, "If I were to listen to James Dickey I would stop writing" (167). Thankfully, she kept on, saying, "When I'm writing, I know I'm doing the thing I was born to do" (Colburn 103).

On gender and mood, Kay Redfield Jamison observes:

> Depression, somehow, is much more in line with society's notions of what women are all about: passive, sensitive, hopeless, helpless, stricken, dependent, confused, rather tiresome, and with limited aspirations. Manic states, on the other hand, seem to be more the provenance of men: restless, fiery, aggressive, volatile, energetic, risk taking, grandiose, and visionary, and impatient with the status quo. (122–123)

Women are expected to wither into their sadness, not act agitated or speak prophetically. They are best kept and vulnerable. Sexton and the aforementioned authors expose the manic side of bipolar disorder. Hornbacher writes,

"I'm telling you I'm losing my mind. I can't take this", I say, pacing in her sunny office, tapping my nails on the walls.... "I can't take these fucking mood swings! It never stops! I'm all over the fucking map!" I fling myself onto the couch, then fling myself up again and pace some more, gripping my head in my hands. (110)

This scene in Hornbacher's therapist's office conveys the boundless energy and fervent frustration of mania. She tells her therapist that she is taking her medication, but it is not reducing the anxiety, the edge. She admits, "I'm not telling her everything. I allude to chaos, mention the drinking, say I'm scared, but I still make light of these things" (110). In withholding the truth, Hornbacher endangers herself, as many with affective disorders do. Jamison asserts that depression "is twice as common in women as men. But manic–depressive illness occurs equally often in women and men" (*Unquiet Mind* 123). Therefore, bipolar women with manic symptoms "are often misdiagnosed, receive poor, if any, psychiatric treatment, and are at high risk for suicide, alcoholism, drug abuse, and violence" (123). The Sextons, Jamison, and Hornbacher admit to abusing alcohol and drugs to cope with their illness, and write about their multiple suicide attempts. Despite self-sabotage, marginalization, and the trepidations of seeking, developing, and maintaining an effective treatment plan, three of these four women are alive and still writing.

The business of words

To treat, manage, and use moods productively is vital to the success of the writer, but few are fortunate enough to have self-awareness and the support to attain this. While in New York on a break from Thorazine, Sexton confided in Dr Orne, "'Quite manic.... If I can pick, I pick this illness (if it is one).' Sexton had experienced the brilliant verbal and emotional energies in July as a pure gift, one she used to attain a new level of art" (Middlebrook 226). Her euphoric tone emanates invincibility as she wonders if she is even ill. It is common for manic patients to refuse or discontinue their medications. Dr Peter C. Whybrow, a psychiatrist and endocrinologist whose research concentrates on bipolar disorder, notes, "The treatment of the creative individual, especially with bipolar disorder, presents unusual clinical challenges.... Those who have experienced the energy and euphoria of hypomania are loath to give them up" ("Of the Muse and Moods Mundane" 478). Sexton chose to risk her wellbeing in order to write and to feel alive, illustrating the desperation

DOI: 10.1057/9781137381668

of her condition. Her illness was acute, so respite from depression was not likely as Thorazine would primarily alter mania and dull her moods, as well as the lust to write. Nonetheless, Sexton remained prolific and earned more money than many poets of the time (Middlebrook 272).

When her mother died, Linda, age 21, became her literary executor; consequently, she stayed close to the turbulence of her mother's cycling moods, first in the flesh and then on the page. She states, "I wanted to be able to rise up someday and spin the straw of my own misery into gold, just the way my mother did. Sadly, I also realized I wanted none of it" (47). Although Linda became a writer who attempted suicide, too, she has instead spun the gold of a survivor's story.

For Marya Hornbacher, writing also means control and potential triumph: "I'm going to be a writer if it kills me. I will kill myself trying, I will get there, I've got to learn it, train for it, write it until the writing is perfect, until I get it, until I make it, I'm going to be real. This time I won't fuck it up. I won't fail" (36). Writing quells the voice self-doubt, provides a focus, a tangible outlet for her obsessive thoughts. Ironically, she "kills" herself in order to write, yet writing well, perfecting the work, will prevent her from killing herself. Under the duress of her disorder, working with words doesn't always work: "Here's the Hell of it: madness doesn't announce itself. There isn't time to prepare for its coming.... But as you learn to manage madness, you begin to notice sooner that it's on its way" (226). For all her preparation, exercise, taking medication and supplements, socializing, keeping a regimen including sufficient sleep, Hornbacher explains that sometimes the tempest arrives anyway, damaging little or obliterating all – its unpredictability makes for exigent composing conditions.

Her kind

In her first memoir, and in her recent book *Half in Love: Surviving the Legacy of Suicide*, Linda Sexton attempts to forgive her mother for the ultimate abandonment of family (especially of children) through suicide. She remembers, "Whether I was two or four, six or ten, whether it was January or July, my mother's mental illness forced her to leave me behind over and over again" (48).

The intrinsic tie between heredity and personality traits like creativity – as well as affective disorders – is evident from clinical studies of adopted children and birth parents. For example, in "Creativity in Manic–Depressives, Cyclothymes, Their Normal Relatives, and

Control Subjects", Andreason and Canter maintain, "one finds a higher prevalence of major affective disorders in the relatives of creative writers than in the relatives of controls" (Richards et al. 281). Mental illness, substance abuse, and suicide were members of Anne Sexton's family. Her biographer confirms that Sexton's grandfather had a stress-induced breakdown, her great aunt ("Nana", a mother-figure to Anne) was institutionalized and received electroshock therapy; her father was formally treated for alcoholism; her mother drank regularly; and one of Anne's sisters would also commit suicide, eventually – not a promising lineage (Middlebrook 4–16). In "The Suicide of Anne Sexton", Dr Herbert Hendin reiterates that her illness is "[characterized by] impulsive sexual behavior with men and women, substance abuse, affective instability, recurrent suicide attempts...and frantic efforts to avoid abandonment" (260–261). Sexton's preoccupation with death, particularly as a way of eliminating any possibility for abandonment – may have been as environmentally inevitable and genetically predisposed as she felt.

Linda Sexton affirms her own "tortured inheritance" of depression that "gnawed away in [her] gut like a wolf in a trap" (3–4). She recalls making preparations after her mother's death: "As my sister and I chose which dress she would be buried in, I resolved never to seek the solution she had found to end her pain" ("In the Shadow"). As Linda approached the age that her mother was when she killed herself, she notes:

> My world fractured in ways I could never have foreseen.... [I] found myself drawn into my own vortex of depression, desperate for relief from the interior pain that obliterated nearly every waking moment.... For the first time in my life, I envied my mother [sic] the solution she had found to quell the pain of her depression.... Finally, I recognized exactly what I had inherited: the lust to sit in the driver's seat of death. ("In the Shadow")

This phrasing relives her mother's suicide by carbon monoxide poisoning in a parked car of their garage. Linda admittedly suffered from depression and abused alcohol, as her mother had. She recounts a painful conversation with her mother: "We never used the word 'crazy' – though when the ambulance arrived...to take her away, the neighborhood children whispered that Mrs. Sexton was nuts again.... 'What does nuts mean?'...[the young Linda wonders.] 'It's just a tiredness in your mind. You rest and then in a while you feel better'" (*Half* 60). A family member's psychological illness breeds anguish and guilt for the child trying to appease her mother's raging moods. Consider what families of those with affective disorders must navigate to maintain a supportive environment, especially post-suicide attempt. Consider, too, how this trauma affects the diagnosed person's identity and sense of self-worth. Linda Sexton wonders, "Would I ever again function as the mother of two, the writer of seven books, the wife of eighteen years?" (126). Here she finds herself inhabiting and defending her mother's same conflicts decades later.

Bees stinging the heart

One August night, alone in my apartment, I collapsed onto the floor. There was a vise grip tightening around my throat and chest. The room darkened, the walls bent, the ceiling buckled. *Am I dying?* My breath was quick and short; my body heaved dread. I was afraid, but of what? *I feel like I'm going crazy.* This was my first, full-blown panic attack induced by sleep deprivation. In 2011, because of too much thyroid medication, I started having heart palpitations, increased anxiety, and weight loss; the sleep disruption became a sapping insomnia that ultimately overloaded my immune system. While I do not have an affective disorder, I have experienced a similar form of mood disruption. Symptoms of Hashimoto's thyroiditis, an autoimmune condition, include mood changes similar to those of cyclothymia, which is "characterized by pronounced but not totally debilitating changes in mood, behavior, sleep, and energy levels ..." (Jamison *Touched* 12). Although I have had emotional vicissitudes before being diagnosed with Hashimoto's, their magnitude and incidence have been drastically altered by my fluctuating thyroid levels.

I have always written, even when I was not mildly depressed or hypomanic. I cannot remember a time without words. My family often described me growing up as the "creative" or "moody" one that was always drawing, making up songs, and inscribing white space. For the past few years, I have been in contact with my birth mother, who is artistic, and takes medication for depression and panic episodes, which prompted me to consider my own predispositions. Diagnosing me is difficult as 1) I have limited genetic history, as I am an adopted child and my biological mother, also adopted, has no access to her history, and 2) My biological father is deceased and I have not had contact with his relatives. Dr Wolkoff, a psychiatrist, explains,

A number of clinical conditions can produce "mental" symptoms, including those of depression or anxiety. Inadequate levels of circulating thyroid hormones lead to a general slowing down including difficulty thinking clearly and frank depressive symptoms. Too much thyroid hormone revs people up in a state sometimes indistinguishable from a hypomanic episode.

When I was diagnosed with hypothyroidism, I was constantly cold and depressed; I could not concentrate, and nearly blacked out at my desk. Once I began Levothyroxine in 2008, my symptoms quickly improved.

Once medicated, I began writing again. Rumination incubated ideas for the works and the medication provided the energy to assemble them. According to Richards et al., "two of the criteria for the hypomanic phase of cyclothymic personality disorder involve sharpened and unusually creative thinking and increased productivity" (282). Like Jamison, "I had...inclined in the direction of exuberant feelings.... These fiery moods were, at least initially, not all bad: in addition to giving a certain romantic tumultuousness to my personal life, they had.... added a great deal that was positive to my professional life.... They had...made me restless for more" (*Unquiet Mind* 122). I feel lucky to have had similar bursts of creative energy throughout my life, which have not incapacitated me, but have more so fostered my writing and academic work.

Magic talking to itself

Madness is a solitary malady, and so is writing.

The human compulsion to make and share meaning transcends culture and climate, gender, and the physical and psychological wellbeing of the author. Nevertheless, the rumination often associated with depression, as well as elevated levels of creativity and productivity associated with mania, do engender significant art in talented individuals – do "[strip] the veil of familiarity from the world", spurring the urgency to record or at least purge that vision (Shelley, qtd. in Leitch et al. 714). In *Touched with Fire*, Jamison examines the episodic or cyclic moods described by artists during the creative process to those highs and lows of diagnosed manic–depressives: "Making connections between opposites [is] crucial to the creative process" as is "melancholy, [which] tends to force a slower pace...and puts into perspective the thoughts, observations, and feelings generated during more enthusiastic moments. Depression prunes and sculpts; it also ruminates and ponders and, ultimately, subdues and focuses thought" (112; 118). Psychologists from Syracuse and Stanford

Universities confirm that one origin of rumination is reduced cognitive inhibition, which "may... contribute to original thinking"; and while rumination and depression are not concomitant exclusively, depression can influence creative process as it "increase[s] introspection" (Verhaeghen et al. 227). Writers, poets especially, concentrate on personal emotions, affecting their creative activity. Yet, as writers are more prone to depression than other artists are, further rumination might worsen their condition; this is a potential contributing factor in Sexton's premature death, along with her focus on first-person lyric poetry, her initial misdiagnosis, and mismanaged medication.

Kaufman and Sexton's studies suggest that female poets are more susceptible to mental illness than male or prose writers because "Women are more likely to use rumination as a form of emotional regulation ..." (272). Depression can impede one's ability to write, further deepening the depression. Anne Sexton admits, "I hate being a writer (when I'm not writing). It's too fucking hard to write... I'd rather be writing something bad than nothing at all!!" (Sexton and Ames 254). Writers of all genres have battled writer's block. "Why Doesn't the Writing Cure Help Poets?" details contrasting physical and emotional effects on authors who composed narrative versus lyric works: "Health improved as measured by days restricted due to illness only for those who wrote in the narrative style" (Kaufman and Sexton 274). Similarly, those who wrote about feelings described more corporal ailments afterward (274). Prose writers have fewer instances of mood fluctuation, as they develop characters and narratives apart from themselves. In contrast, poets ponder and then attempt to encapsulate nuances of emotion in condensed language, slowing the work to a brief moment in time; as a result, they seem more susceptible to mood disruption.

If rumination can facilitate a writer's ability to gestate and edit works if the depression is not incapacitating, how does mania influence the process? According to Jamison, "Hypomania and mania often generate ideas and associations, propel contact with life and other people, induce frenzied energies and enthusiasms, and cast an ecstatic, rather cosmic hue over life" (*Touched* 118). While off her medication, Sexton's zeal intensified: "if the magic only comes around every 5 or 6 years, I've got to use it, just got to." [Middlebrook asks,] "*Was* insanity the root of 'Language'? Would Thorazine eliminate the magic?" (227). Mania fueled the poet's productivity during the winter of 1973 when she again stopped taking Thorazine, and in 20 days composed 39 poems, the draft for *The Awful Rowing Toward God* (366).

Undoubtedly, in the arms of mania writing comes effortlessly. Words and ideas, flawless images fall into the mind from nowhere, and the manic writer atop that precipice is in love with every one of them. The editor is easy to ignore. Everything makes sense, all is meaningful, connected, sparkling, intensely beautiful; it must be captured, seized at its most lush moment, lest its essence diminish. As Hornbacher puts it, there is a "cyclone of words". She describes a manic fever: "I'm sitting in the study lounge, it's five A.M., and I have no idea how many nights or days have gone by since I last slept. I'm starving, I'm writing, I can't stop, don't want to stop, don't want to eat, I am possessed by words.... I'm going to stay awake forever if I have to, just so long as I write this, whatever it is" (35). The genre, academic essays or short stories, is irrelevant. The only thing that matters is to keep going, to push into words, to make sense of the too-quick searing flashes of thought that emblaze her mind; to feel that alive, that engaged and cogent becomes a passion. Anything can seem life altering, astonishing from inside of mania, but the exactitude and control required for laborious revision and editing harbors the author to the ground once more. The multifaceted work of creating, of manipulating language, gives essential purpose to the writer. According to researchers at Harvard Medical School and The Psychological Institute, Copenhagen: "It is noteworthy that eminent artists and writers have described hypomanic symptomology during intense creative periods ... and that manics and hypomanics have attributed both immediate and lasting effects on creativity to hypomanic states" (Richards et al. 287). Manic–depressive illness, they believe, may benefit creativeness in "those individuals who are relatively better functioning", dispelling the myth that all mad artists embody genius (281). To a novice poet, Sexton replies, "Hell! I'm undisciplined too, in everything but my work ... and the discipline the reworking the forging into being is the stuff of poetry [sic]. ... Madness is a waste of time. It creates nothing .... I fight it because ... nothing grows from it and you, meanwhile, only grow into it like a snail" (267). Sexton diligently wrote, sometimes for nine or more hours a day, revising some poems hundreds of time, and imparted her strict methods to her students and fledgling poets seeking advice (Colburn 88–111). Her admission that "madness ... creates nothing" strikes with ethos: she knows well the way her illness could impede her craft. The work, discipline, and self-care make writing possible; moods only propel parts of the process. Dr Peter C. Whybrow believes, "[For those whose] illness is severe, the

DOI: 10.1057/9781137381668

balance of evidence suggests that the creative process will be improved with [proper] treatment. After all, creativity... is fundamental to all human achievement, even recovery from illness" ("Of the Muse and Moods Mundane" 478).

In *An Unquiet Mind*, Jamison reminds us, "Manic–depression is a disease that both kills and gives life. Fire, by its nature, both creates and destroys" (123). For Sexton and many others, this is true regarding not only the physical life but also the life of their words. The final works rise as a phoenix from the ashes of creative process, thriving where the body no longer survives. Writing meant fleeting freedom from the seemingly inexpressible and destructive ideas that churned in Sexton's subconscious. If she had not turned to poetry, dragging the essence of conflict into existence and making it lucid in literary form, her readers would be deprived of her insight regarding familial and interpersonal relationships, idealizations of women, and the stigmas of mental illness and suicide. As Sexton once said about teaching poetry workshops at McLean Hospital, where she was previously institutionalized, "Poetry led me by the hand out of madness. I am hoping I can show others that route" (Middlebrook 309). Admirably, she had come to terms with her purpose through writing: to help others make sense of themselves and the world. Linda Gray Sexton, Kay Redfield Jamison, and Marya Hornbacher are continuing her essential work.

The words of these authors trap mercurial temperaments and candidly consider adverse relationships with the body, our common text. I return to and teach their writing because it is necessary. Ultimately, the achievement of writing with and about affective disorders remains educating others about how to cope with symptoms and how to facilitate a network of support between therapists, relatives, and friends. Above all, opening the insular world of patients and encouraging them to disclose their experiences will lift stigma. Literature is tuned to a resounding universal note: *not alone*. Really, this is what most writers, touched or well, want of the work: to know that it resonates long after we are gone, long after the ink has cracked the frozen sea of each barren page.

Works cited

"Anne Sexton: Biography". *Poetryfoundation.org*. Poetry Foundation. n.d. Web. 10 June 2012.

"Bipolar Disorder". *Psych.org.* American Psychiatric Association. Web. 18 June 2012.
Colburn, Steven, ed. *No Evil Star: Selected Essays, Interviews, and Prose [of] Anne Sexton.* Ann Arbor: Michigan UP, 1985. Print.
"Cyclothymic Disorder". Proposed Revision for DSM-5. *Psych.org.* American Psychiatric Association. 26 April 2012. Web. 18 June 2012.
Dickey, James. Review of *To Bedlam and Part Way Back*. In Colburn, Stephen. Ed. *Anne Sexton: Telling the Tale.* Ann Arbor: U of Michigan Press, 1988.
Hendin, Herbert. "The Suicide of Anne Sexton". *Suicide and Life-Threatening Behavior*, Fall 1993. 23(2): 257+. New York: Guilford. *Health Reference Center Academic.* Web. 18 June 2012.
Hornbacher, Marya. *Madness: A Bipolar Life.* 2008. Boston: Mariner/Houghton Mifflin Harcourt, 2009. Print.
Jamison, Kay Redfield. *An Unquiet Mind: A Memoir of Moods and Madness.* 1995. New York: Vintage Books/Random House, 1996. Print.
——. *Touched with Fire: Manic–Depressive Illness and the Artistic Temperament.* 1993. New York: Simon & Schuster, 1994. Print.
Jong, Erica. "Remembering Anne Sexton". *The New York Times.* 27 October 1974. Web. 20 July 2012.
Kaufman, James C. and Janel D. Sexton. "Why Doesn't the Writing Cure Help Poets?" *Review of General Psychology* 10.3 (2006): 268–282. *PsycInfo.* Web. 8 July 2012.
Kumin, Maxine. Introduction. *Anne Sexton: The Complete Poems.* Boston: Houghton Mifflin, 1981. Print.
McClatchy, J.D., ed. *Anne Sexton: The Artist and Her Critics.* Bloomington: Indiana UP, 1978. Print.
Middlebrook, Diane Wood. *Anne Sexton: A Biography.* 1991. New York: Vintage/Random House, 1992. Print.
Richards, Ruth et al. "Creativity in Manic–Depressives, Cyclothymes, Their Normal Relatives, and Control Subjects". *Journal of Abnormal Psychology*, 1988. 97(3): 281–288. *Health Reference Center Academic.* Web. 8 July 2012.
Sexton, Linda Gray, ed. *The Complete Poems: Anne Sexton.* Boston: Houghton Mifflin, 1981. Print.
Sexton, Anne. "You, Doctor Martin". Sexton, Linda Gray. Ed. *The Complete Poems: Anne Sexton.* Boston: Houghton Mifflin, 1981. 3–4. Print.
——. "Music Swims Back to Me". Sexton, Linda Gray. 6–7.
——. "Flee on Your Donkey". Sexton, Linda Gray. 97–105.

——. "Wanting to Die". Sexton, Linda Gray. 142–143.
Sexton, Linda Gray and Lois Ames, eds *Anne Sexton: A Self-Portrait in Letters*. Boston: Houghton Mifflin, 1977. Print.
Sexton, Linda Gray. *Half in Love: Surviving the Legacy of Suicide*. Berkeley: Counterpoint, 2011. Print.
——. "In the Shadow of My Mother's Suicide". *Salon.com*. 8 January 2011. Web. 9 March 2012.
——. "A Tortured Inheritance". *The New York Times: Op Ed*. 9 April 2009. Web. 9 March 2012.
Shelly, Percy Bysshe. "A Defense of Poetry". *The Norton Anthology of Theory and Criticism*. Ed. Vincent B. Leitch et al. New York: W.W. Norton, 2001. 699–717. Print.
Thomas, Katherine M. and Marshall Duke. "Depressed Writing: Cognitive Distortions in the Works of Depressed and Nondepressed Poets and Writers". *Psychology of Aesthetics, Creativity, and the Arts*, 2007. 1(4): 204–218. *PsycInfo*. Web. 10 July 2012.
Verhaeghen, Paul, et al. "Why We Sing the Blues: The Relation Between Self-Reflective Rumination, Mood, and Creativity". *Emotion*, 2005. 5(2): 226–232. *PsycInfo*. Web. 8 July 2012.
Wolkoff, Irvin. "Medical Conditions Can often Mimic Emotional Disorders". *The Toronto Star: Your Mind, Life Section*. 23 April 1999. *LexisNexis*. Web. 30 May 2012.
Whybrow, Peter C. "Of the Muse and Moods Mundane". *The American Journal of Psychiatry*, April 1994. 151(4): 477–478. *ProQuest*. Web. 18 June 2012.

Works consulted

Friedan, Betty. *The Feminine Mystique*. 1963. New York: W.W. Norton & Co., 1997. Print.
George, Diana Hume. "Anne Sexton's Suicide Poems". *Critical Essays on Anne Sexton*. Ed. Linda Wagner-Martin. Boston: G.K. Hall, 1989. Print.
Jamison, Kay Redfield. *Night Falls Fast: Understanding Suicide*. New York: Vintage/Random House, 1999. Print.
Kecmanović, Dušan. "Somatic Diseases and Mental Disorders: Should They Be Differentiated?" *Acta Medica Academica*, 2006. 35: 94–106. Web. *Academic Search Complete*. 20 July 2012.

Lindamood, Wes. "Thorazine". *Chemical & Engineering News*. American Chemical Society. 2005. Web. 10 June 2012.

Ludwig, Arnold M. "Mental Illness and Creative Activity in Female Writers". *The American Journal of Psychiatry*, November 1994. 151(11): 1650–1656. Proquest. Web. 10 June 2012.

Swenson, Rand S. "Limbic System: Chapter 9". *Review of Clinical and Functional Neuroscience*. Dartmouth Medical School. Web. 10 June 2012.

Whybrow, Peter C. "Mood Swings". *Saturday Evening Post*, 2005. 277(4): 36–86. Ebsco. Web. 24 July 2012.

7
The Things We Carry: Embodied Truth and Tim O'Brien's Poetics of Despair

David Bahr

Abstract: *Bahr examines O'Brien's* The Things They Carried*, a work often categorized as postmodern, and shows how this fractured, unstable, and contradictory text mirrors the physiological experience of trauma and mental illness, phenomenologically conveying the subjectivity of its author. He terms the text an "aesthetic autobiography", which repositions "aesthetic" in its ancient Greek context, meaning to apprehend by the senses. Drawing on Ross Chambers' concepts of "phantom pain" and "orphaned memory", Bahr introduces the idea of "orphaned pain" and presents how O'Brien's text has become a surrogate autobiography of what Bahr, a former foster child with a mentally ill mother, has struggled to articulate in his own life: the embodied despair resulting from extreme events.*

Keywords: Trauma; memory; mental illness; phantom pain; Tim O'Brien

Horton, Stephanie Stone, ed. *Affective Disorder and the Writing Life: The Melancholic Muse.* Basingstoke: Palgrave Macmillan, 2014. DOI: 10.1057/9781137381668.

> Legally accredited truth is one thing – the truth of a life is another.
>
> Bruno Dossekker as "Binjamin Wilkomirski", in the "Afterword"
> of *Fragments: Memoirs of a Wartime Childhood*

In 1994, Tim O'Brien reflected on his psychological state in a *New York Times Magazine* article, "The Vietnam in Me", two decades after leaving the war:

> Last night suicide was on my mind. Not whether, but how. Tonight it will be on my mind again. Now it's 4 A.M., June the 5th. The sleeping pills have not worked. I sit in my underwear at this unblinking fool of a computer and try to wrap words around a few horrid truths. (50)

It was not the first time O'Brien had written about Vietnam and his despair. Twenty years earlier, he had published a memoir, *If I Die in a Combat Zone*, about his experiences as a drafted soldier in the war. And, in 1990, after two novels on the subject, *Northern Lights* (1975) and *Going After Cacciato* (1978), he published a genre-defying work of auto-biographical fiction, *The Things They Carried*. As with the three books preceding it, *The Things They Carried* is informed by O'Brien's time in the military. While *If I Die* and *Going After Cacciato* depict the theater of war, and *Northern Lights* examines a veteran's return, *The Things They Carried* is alternately set during, before, and after its protagonist, Tim O'Brien, is deployed to Vietnam. (Throughout this chapter, I refer to the narrator as "Tim" and to the author as "O'Brien".) Understandably, it is within the context of the Vietnam War that literary scholars often discuss *The Things They Carried*, frequently by connecting Vietnam, postmodernism, and meta-fiction (Bates 1996; Chen 1998; Jarraway 1998; Neilson 2001; Carpenter 2003; Haswell 2004; Kaufmann 2005; Silbergleid 2009).

Although I have never been in combat or the military, I feel a strong emotional connection to the work. Because of *The Things They Carried*, I have reconsidered my own relationship to autobiography, truth, and language, particularly in regard to my painful past as a foster child with a mentally ill mother. Like many critics, I view *The Things They Carried* as postmodern, in that it is intentionally unstable, fractured, "schizophrenic", in a Deleuzian sense. This schizophrenia – for example, its "polyphonic" perspectives and conspicuous contradictions – keeps the text in play. The book is what I term an aesthetic autobiography, in which I reposition "aesthetic" in its ancient Greek context, meaning to apprehend by the senses. As an aesthetic autobiography, *The Things They*

Carried phenomenologically conveys the subjectivity of its author and has become a surrogate autobiography of what I have struggled to articulate in my own life: the embodied despair resulting from extreme events. My own experience with anxiety and low-grade depression (clinically known as dysthymia) suggests that traumatic events, a biological predisposition, as well as habits of mind and behavior all play a dynamic but unquantifiable part. I can only vouch for how aesthetic works like *The Things They Carried* have helped me manage and alleviate these bouts. In formally expressing what had previously been solely sensed, they reconnect me with the world and animate my writing, affirming a vital reciprocity between the individual and the collective in the creative realm.

The Things They Carried as a meta-fictive work of war

In "The Undying Uncertainty of the Narrator in Tim O'Brien's *The Things They Carried*" (1993), one of the first scholarly articles on O'Brien's book, Steven Kaplan quotes Wolfgang Iser to contextualize O'Brien's work: "literature is not an explanation of origins; it is a staging of the constant deferment of explanation" (47). Kaplan anticipates later readings that explicitly identify O'Brien's book as a postmodern text (Herzog). Yet, according to Fredric Jameson, postmodernism "is not merely contested, it is also internally conflicted and contradictory" (xxii). As Linda Hutcheon writes, in postmodernism's "extreme formulation, the result is that consensus becomes the illusion of consensus" (7). Still, Hutcheon offers a working "definition" that I find useful here: "what I want to call postmodernism is fundamentally contradictory, resolutely historical, and inescapably political ... but whatever the cause, these contradictions are certainly manifest in the important postmodern concept of 'the presence of the past'" (4). The idea of a "present past" is a compelling paradox. It rings especially true in terms of embodied "memories". I understand embodied memories as a physiological déjà vu in which sensations associated with a past event are triggered by certain sounds, smells, images, and patterns. As someone whose childhood was serially and abruptly ruptured by a mentally ill mother who could not care for me, I can experience triggered flashes of dread and unaccountable harm. During such moments, my heart races, I may perspire, become nauseous, and develop a slight fever. Of course, embodied memories, those both disturbing and delightful, are not necessarily uncommon or extreme. Yet for the traumatized and mentally ill, embodied memories, which are non-narrative and elude clear and definite conceptualization, the stakes are higher. Trauma and depression can isolate individuals. A desire and accompanying failure to communicate physiological experiences can amplify feelings of disconnection and despair. The postmodern – as fractured, unstable, and contradictory – mirrors the physiological experience of trauma and mental illness in crucial ways. Hutcheon notes that the postmodern "perceiving subject is no longer assumed to be a coherent, meaning-generating entity"; "narrators in [postmodern] fiction become either disconcertingly multiple and hard to locate" (11). As a former traumatized child who has struggled with anxiety and low-grade depression, I find the fractured self both comprehensible and identifiable.

In *Metafiction: The Theory and Practice of Self-Conscious Fiction* (1984), Patricia Waugh defines metafiction as writing that "self-consciously... draws attention to its status as an artefact in order to pose questions about the relationship between fiction and reality" (2). With the ability "to 'describe' anything" compromised, all literary fiction can do is "represent" discourses (4). Language "becomes a 'prisonhouse' from which the possibility of escape is remote", and metafiction explores this "dilemma" (4). Waugh's definition of metafiction anticipates O'Brien's exploration of that "dilemma" in regard to presenting historical, biographical, and phenomenological "truth", particularly when that truth is emotionally painful.

Playing on the ambiguity of "truth", Tim states that there is "story-truth" and "happening-truth" (*Things* 203). As he puts it, a "story-truth" feels true, but a "happening-truth" is a factual occurrence. The first is the realm of the subjective. Here, I note a paradox: that a subjective, felt "story-truth" is also a factual occurrence. Embodied responses are real, although such "truths" are shifting, dynamic, and not easily, if at all, conceptually conveyed. On the other hand, as Tim puts it, a "happening-truth" concerns objective facts. For him, a happening truth is the Vietnam War. For me, happening truths would include: at 18 months old, I was left at a foundling hospital by my mentally ill mother; I was placed into foster care at age two; my mother reclaimed me five years later; she left me at the children's psychiatric hospital at Mount Sinai when I was ten; six months later, I was transferred to Pleasantville Cottage School for troubled youth. These are documented facts. But many more details concerning these facts are not documented, nor can I recall them. Further, my feelings at the time of these events are difficult to locate. All I have are memories, a dynamic interplay of sensations and images, which only exist in the present. To compound this situation, I admit to not having the best memory for details or "happening truths". I often insist that something occurred, although others may dispute it; I am later proven wrong. When I look back at journal entries (and I am neither a rigorous nor dedicated diarist), I am frequently surprised by the person that I was. My subjective truth is often relative and shifting, which is why, for me, "postmodernism" feels true. For O'Brien, and myself, the imbrication of "story truth" and "happening truth" is not an untenable paradox but the nature of our being. Haswell notes, "What O'Brien offers (and what critics affirm) is not a report of the war, but a 'rehappening' shaped by memory and imagination, making story-telling or writing itself on par with the war as the subject of the collection" (95). In other words, *The Things They Carried* is not about the politics of war (although the text is informed by politics); rather, it is about O'Brien's subjective, embodied experience and how he employs language to convey the sensational.

Critics such as Andrew Martin, Renny Christopher, and Jim Nielson are justifiably concerned that a focus on subjectivity, instability, and provisionality overshadows the socioeconomic and political realities that led to and defined the war. They also are uneasy – as I am – with any form of intellectualization that erases the feeling, embodied subject. In the postmodern age, a unified conceptual subject may no longer be viable but the embodied subject is real and locatable, if not fixed. A person in pain exceeds language. And while there are those who may view *The Things They Carried* as a postmodern language "game", I have never experienced the book in such a strict cerebral context. It is a work of intelligence, but it is also a product of profound feeling. It is an aesthetic autobiography in which O'Brien explores the formal "dilemma" of conveying the phenomenology of embodied trauma and depression.

Good form

The Things They Carried is a work of 22 separately titled "chapters". They alternate between longer "stories" able to stand alone and shorter pieces that comment on and connect the lengthier texts. Yet, it is "Good Form" – number 18 in the sequence and about a page long – to which critics often refer when analyzing the form of the entire work. Robin Silbergleid states that "Good Form" is "like a piece of nonfiction, an essay about O'Brien's writing process" that "encourages us to read it as a fairly didactic discussion of how and why Tim O'Brien does what he does" (145). The narrator of "Good Form" states that he is "forty-three years old", "a writer", and was once a foot soldier in Vietnam. "Almost everything else is invented", he adds. "Right here, now, as I invent myself, I'm thinking of all I want to tell you about why this book is written as it is" (O'Brien, *Things* 203). The narrator proceeds to describe a man he saw die but then states that the story is made up. Such assertion and denial is not mean to be "game", the narrator explains, but "a form" (203). "I want you to feel what I felt", he states. "I want you to know why story-truth is truer sometimes than happening-truth" (203). Not everyone appreciates O'Brien's artful equivocating. In his *Wall Street Journal* review, Bruce Bawer calls the book "overly disingenuous" (qtd in Herzog 896) and criticizes O'Brien for "playing too many such fact-or-fiction games" (914). Similarly, Herzog recalls attending a reading by O'Brien in which the author casually recounted a seemingly autobiographical story about how he decided to go to Vietnam after nearly fleeing to Canada. At the end, however, O'Brien admitted that the story was invented. According to Herzog, a number of veterans felt betrayed by the "deception" (O'Brien simply retold from memory the story "On the Rainy River", which appears in *The Things They Carried*.) I can see why Bawer finds O'Brien's technique off-putting: the instability between "fact" and "fiction" *is* unnerving. I especially understand why the veterans were upset: I might be distressed to hear a writer who wrote autobiographically about being a foster child tell a story presented as fact conclude with "but that never happened". Yet, regardless of the writer's biography, I think that I would recognize whether he had "gotten it", whether the story felt true to my lived experience. So when Tim states, "I want you to feel what I felt", "I want you to know why story-truth is truer sometimes than happening-truth", I understand. I know what it feels like to be at a loss for the facts because I do not have historical records, my memories are too painful, or I cannot recall events. I know how the imagination fills in gaps with "fictions" that become "true".

Ross Chambers explores how fiction becomes an embodied truth with his concepts of "phantom pain", "orphaned memory", and "foster writing". Chambers draws on the 1995 publication, and subsequent recall three years later, of the "faux" memoir *Fragments*, by a German writer named "Binjamin Wilkomirski". Wilkomirski claimed to be an orphaned Jewish Auschwitz survivor. It was later revealed that he was actually a Swiss orphan and foster child named Bruno Doessekker. Chambers writes "in experiencing Wilkomirski's pain as his own, Doessekker the man transforms his personal sense of orphanhood into the experience of a 'phantom' pain; and that his writing then functions as a mode of transmission for the painful Wilkomirski memories that derive from the collective memory but that he takes as his own, in such a way that they become phantom pain in the minds of his book's readers" (101). Chambers derives the term "phantom pain" from "the neurophysiological phenomenon whereby people who have lost a limb experience a sensation of physical pain in the amputated extremity" (102). Phantom pain explains "the capacity to experience the pain of another, or of others, as wholly or partly indistinguishable from a 'remembered' pain of one's own" (102). An "orphaned memory", however, is a memory without a locus. It is, as Chambers puts it, "a kind of visitation" (102) originating in a collective memory and conveyed through its host, the foster writer. In *Fragments*, the persona of Wilkomirski is the orphan memory, a visitation of collective suffering, whereas Dossekker is the foster writer and his "memoir" an example of foster writing.

Orphaned memories belong to a communal memory of events "that we had forgotten, denied, or ignored" (108). To experience phantom pain, a reader need only possess "the capacity to experience the pain of another, or of others, as wholly or partly indistinguishable from a 'remembered' pain of one's own" (108). Chambers writes: "I need only to recognize its reality and relate it to myself, which presumably I do on the basis of personal experiences of pain that I remember" (108). In other words, this "recognized" pain belongs to a sensational, embodied logic outside of cognitive reasoning and understanding. It is felt. What I like about orphaned memories and phantom pain is their relational dynamic. They explain the role that storytelling plays in forging affective communities. As Tim states in "Good Form", what stories "can do, I guess, is make things present. I can look at things I never looked at. I can attach faces to grief and love and pity and God. I can be brave. I can make myself feel again" (O'Brien, *Things* 204).

Making the stomach believe

"How to Tell a True War Story" is the seventh "chapter" in *The Things They Carried*, but it is arguably the most representative example of O'Brien's "schizoid" approach described in "Good Form". Tim's insistent assertions ("This is true") and counter-assertions resemble the process of memory, which is always reshaping, recontextualizing, revising. Stories are for "when you can't remember how you got from where you were to where you are", "when there is nothing to remember except the story" (40). For Tim, you remember the story when you cannot remember the facts. Stories become our memory and, in turn, our "facts". Of the actual event, on which stories are based, "pictures get jumbled; you tend to miss a lot. And then afterward, when you go to tell about it, there is always that surreal seemingness, which makes the story seem untrue, but which in fact represents the hard and exact truth as it seemed" (78). I identify with this "surreal seemingness" of painful events. When I tell strangers how my mother left me at a psychiatric hospital when I was ten, the story always surprises me, as if it were someone else's life. Each retelling recontextualizes it, making the story feel both familiar and strange. I can imagine how, for those with more extreme stories, the disjuncture between event and retelling would be greater.

"How to Tell a True War Story" is a series of anecdotal fragments about the death of a fellow soldier. Throughout the text, Tim interrupts the "story" with reflexive commentary and narrative theorizing. The incommunicable loss of the soldier culminates in the chapter's final, oft-cited anecdote: the brutal killing of a baby buffalo. This account of random vengeance is Tim's attempt to get at a "truth" that "makes the stomach believe" (84). Yet the anecdote, like all the others within the chapter, is framed by failure: "All you can do is tell it one more time, patiently, adding and subtracting, making up a few things to get at the real truth... you just keep on telling it" (91). The buffalo tale is not presented to help the reader understand Tim's experience of violent loss (he does not even comprehend it); nor is it meant to help the reader visualize Vietnam. Rather, the story is a phenomenological account of Tim's embodied brutalization and despair. He wants us to feel it.

"How to Tell a True War Story", like all the pieces in the book, is not an account of the past; it is an account of the past as a present "rehappening". The pain of this "rehappening" is embodied, yet, as the recollected events become increasingly surreal and estranging, the pain has no clear locus. It is "orphaned". Storytelling temporally grounds and objectifies such pain. Orphan pain, as I conceive the term, is distinct from Chambers' concept of orphan memories, which are collective narratives that have no originating host, and phantom pain, which is the appropriation of another's pain. Orphan pain is a fairly steady, if intermittent, presence in the body that loses its context because the narratives associated with it either have become exhausted or lost. New narratives are constructed and revised to justify the pain. The fifth *O.E.D.* definition of "justify" is relevant here: "to confirm or support by attestation or evidence; to corroborate, prove, verify". As a relational act, storytelling affectively connects people through such justification.

For me, a story that powerfully justifies orphaned pain as a source of potential identification and connection is "Speaking of Courage", more than halfway through the book. In this piece, set during July 4, a soldier named Norman Bowker suffers from post-traumatic stress disorder and has trouble re-assimilating to civilian life. Feeling as if he does not belong anywhere – either "home" or in the war – he drives around the lake of his town, imagining conversations with the living and the dead. "Invisible in the soft twilight" (O'Brien, *Things* 169), Bowker looks to strangers, like a female carhop at a fast-food drive-in, but he is unable to connect. "Dark was pressing in tight now, and he wished there were somewhere to go" (170). But there isn't. Bowker continues to circle the lake and then gets out of the car after a "twelfth revolution" as the sky goes "crazy with color"; he dips his head in the water, suggesting a baptism, a cleansing, and the promise of hope.

Milton Bates has stated that "Speaking of Courage" is "a model of the well-wrought short story" notable for its "symmetries"; in the next chapter, however, "the symmetry comes undone" (250). That section, entitled "Notes", as Silbergleid has observed, "reads like a piece of nonfiction" (139). "Notes" begins: "'Speaking of Courage' was written in 1975 at the suggestion of Norman Bowker, who three years later hanged himself" (O'Brien, *Things* 177). Silbergleid observes how "Notes" "isn't actually nonfiction but adopts the rhetorical devices of essay writing" (139). I first read "Notes" in preparation for an interview I did with O'Brien. I believed his gloss on "Speaking of Courage" as a statement of fact, yet, during our conversation, the issue of what was fact and fiction arose. At the time, it mattered to me what was and was not historically true. I recall that he claimed that the entire book was fabricated except for the suicide of an army buddy, which had prompted him to write "Speaking of Courage" and "Notes". When I later read the interview in which O'Brien stated that "Notes" was also a fiction, I felt betrayed. Over time, like Silbergleid, I have come to realize that whether Bowker's story actually happened is irrelevant. Both the story and its proposed autobiographical context feel emotionally true to me. According to the narrator of "Notes", the impetus for the story was "a long, disjointed letter in which Bowker described the problem of finding a meaningful use for his life after the war" (O'Brien,

Things 177). The "real" Bowker lived with his parents and held a series of short-term, menial jobs. He enrolled in a local community college but the class work "seemed too abstract, too distant, with nothing real or tangible at stake" (177), so he dropped out. He spent mornings in bed, played basketball, and drove around alone. Fact or fiction, such alienation is identifiable to me. Not only traumatized soldiers may recognize the problem "of finding a meaningful use" for one's life, of doing what is socially expected and logical but achieving no traction, of spending "mornings in bed", and finding oneself "mostly alone" (177). These two chapters speak to my own "capacity to experience the pain of another" as "indistinguishable from a 'remembered' pain". For me, and I would contend O'Brien, these vehicles of phantom pain justify our orphan pain.

The sensations fostered by these stories derive not only from the images but also from the author's style. Throughout "Speaking of Courage", O'Brien employs extended clauses and recursive cadences. I am referring to the sensation of lyricism: its musicality, its rhythm and tone, particularly when conveying despair. Although lyricism has its negative associations – for example, affectation or sentimentality – its harmonious qualities can foster a feeling of congruity and connection. In O'Brien's case, the rhythm of his prose harmonizes the stark, isolated experience of suicidal despair. The opening paragraph of "Speaking of Courage" establishes a psychological and topographical setting: "Norman Bowker followed the tar road on its seven-mile loop around the lake", although there is "no place in particular to go" (157). O'Brien takes Bowker and the reader on a slow, lulling tour through a somnolent town. The "houses were all low-slung", "the lawns were spacious", and the "lake lay flat and silvery against the sun" (157). This is a realm of capacious stillness. O'Brien has an affinity for lists; the syntax rolls fluently along with nouns and phrases joined by the conjunction "and". The alliteration and diphthongs produce an aural lullaby. It is the language of a daydreamer adrift in melancholy, just beyond the grasp of paralyzing despair.

In "Speaking of Courage", the rhythmic descriptions dominate the piece; when dialogue intervenes, it is a dissonant rupture. Bowker's encounter with a fast-food attendant, and his brief, disconnected exchange with a female carhop, are his first conversations with people that are not imagined. The dialogue's sharp, staccato rhythm contrasts with the mostly euphonic narration, amplifying Bowker's uneasy interaction with the world beyond his imagination. When O'Brien writes, "he ate quickly, without looking up" (170), it is a poignant moment of unbridgeable isolation. The pathos is intensified with the return to lyricism: "Dark was pressing in tight now, and he wished there were somewhere to go." After a twelfth orbit, Bowker stops the car "in the shadow of a picnic shelter" (173), and O'Brien brings this story to a close. Bowker wades into the lake, feels the "water warm against his skin" and submerges his head, opening "his lips, very slightly, for the taste", then stands and watches the colorful pyrotechnics. There is a romance to "Speaking of Courage", culminating in temporary purchase. But the redemption is slight and ephemeral, located in water and fleeting fireworks.

"Notes" dispels any promise of salvation. The blunt syntax suggests the "truths" of a hardened reporter. Alone, "Speaking of Courage" possesses a wistfulness buoyed by fragile optimism. In relation to "Notes", that sentiment attains a darker cast, showcasing the limits of poetic language. Ultimately, any reconciliation that "Speaking of Courage" offers is through the writing process. In "Notes", O'Brien/Tim states that writing the story guided him "through a swirl of memories that might otherwise have ended in paralysis or worse" (179). Jeff Loeb notes how the intellectual engagement with literary texts often tend to "lose or dismiss an important component ... of the narrative project: the human being behind the story" (96). For those chronicling their emotional pain, the embodied "human being behind the story" needs to be acknowledged. The human being behind "Speaking of Courage" and "Notes" is Tim O'Brien, who also is the author of the autobiographical essay "The Vietnam in Me". In that *Times*' piece, O'Brien confesses to suicidal thoughts and tells of having spent around 9,000 dollars in treatment for depression ("Vietnam" 51–52). As a result, Bowker is more than a symbol of the suicidal soldier; he has an affective genesis in O'Brien himself. As his recursive themes reveal, writing is how O'Brien handles his embodied memories and orphaned pain.

Writing as a mode of living defines O'Brien's final chapter, "The Lives of the Dead". An episodic narrative, frequently photographic in its effect, the piece shifts between scenes of war, childhood, and the present. Stylistically, it combines the metafiction of "How to Tell a True War Story" with the lyrical realism of "Speaking of Courage". Once again, O'Brien begins with "truth": "this too is true: stories can save us" (*Things* 255). But "salvation" is not what "The Lives of the Dead" is finally about. Rather, the work concerns writing as a living process, what Elaine Scarry calls "the objectifying power of the imagination" (164). As Tim states: "By telling stories, you objectify your own experience. You separate it from yourself" (O'Brien, *Things* 179). "The Lives of the Dead" begins in 1990 when Tim is "forty-three years, and a writer now", "dreaming" through storytelling (255). His memories turn to the Vietnam War. He recalls his first encounter with a dead body, and how, through language, the more seasoned soldiers kept death at a distance by conversing with corpses. These memories transport Tim to 1956 and his first childhood sweetheart, Linda, who, we learn, has cancer. Linda lives through the summer but is dead before the fall. Throughout "The Lives of the Dead", O'Brien shifts among these three periods of Tim's life, playing the memories off each other. Storytelling, an act of dreaming, keeps the dead, like Linda, "alive". "I can revive, at least briefly, that which is absolute and unchanging", Tim explains (265). Yet, throughout *The Things They Carried*, O'Brien has undermined any stable identity. If there is anything "absolute and unchanging", it is not found in the conceptual but phenomenological "self".

In "The Vietnam in Me", O'Brien recounts his return to Vietnam in 1994, with his younger girlfriend, Kate. It is his first visit to the country since the war. Like "The Lives of the Dead", the essay shifts back and forth in time. He recalls his return, the awakened memories, and his attempt to write the piece as he battles depression after his break-up with Kate. The essay becomes a chronicle of his struggle with "despair" (51). "This is a valence of horror that Vietnam never approximated", he writes. "If war is hell, what do we call hopelessness?" (51). He notes that "I have not killed myself... maybe tomorrow" because, like "Nam, it goes" (51). To keep suicidal depression at bay, O'Brien takes walks, works out, composes lists, calls friends, visits lawyers, buys furniture, and keeps his "eyes off the sleeping pills" (53). His struggle is ongoing. "Numerous times over the past several days, at least a dozen, this piece has come close to hyperspace", O'Brien writes of the essay. "Twice it lay at the bottom of a wastebasket" (53). The reference to hyperspace – which in non-Euclidean geometry indicates a relativist space–time continuum – is compelling. Writing can make the past come alive, serving as a kind of time travel, but the effect is double-edged. As revealed in "How To Tell a True War Story", the need to write in order to anchor orphan pain, which haunts the body because its source is forgotten, exhausted, or not locatable, can result in a repetition compulsion that fosters pain. Writing, as O'Brien has stated, is not about "escaping" but "dealing" with "the real world" (Schroeder, "Two Interviews" 138). For a depressed individual, writing can be a means of moving from a state of paralysis to reengagement. But revived memories can also kindle pain. In O'Brien's case, painful memories have a physiological stranglehold on him. His only recourse is to "move or die" (O'Brien, "Vietnam" 56). Writing, which is active, is movement.

Writing may animate a writer, reconnecting him with the phenomenal world. But a written work also has the potential to sensationally connect readers. "The thing about a story is that you dream it as you tell it, hoping that others might then dream along with you" (*Things* 259), Tim says. "All you can do is wait" and "hope somebody'll pick it up and start reading" (273). I did not pick up *The Things They Carried* until I was assigned to interview O'Brien. I had categorized the work as a "war book" and did not think it would speak to me, much less move me. But, it did both, powerfully. And right now, as I write, I am close enough in age to O'Brien when he composed the following passage, which I have read numerous times, to myself and my students.

> It's now 1990. I'm forty three years old, which would've seemed impossible to a fourth grader, and yet when I look at photographs of myself as I was in 1956, I realize that in the important ways I haven't changed at all. I was Timmy then; now I'm Tim. But the essence remains the same. I'm not fooled by the baggy pants or the crewcut or the happy smile – I know my own eyes – and there is no doubt that the Timmy smiling at the camera is the Tim I am now. Inside the body, or beyond the body, there is something absolute and unchanging. (264–265)

Looking at the author photo of O'Brien on the back of my book, I cannot help but imagine a fourth-grade Tim, conflating the author and protagonist as O'Brien has encouraged the reader to do. But the picture that I ultimately see is not the fourth-grade O'Brien. It is a first-grade picture of me, at age seven, just before I was taken from my foster family by my mother. The photo captures a boy who does not yet know what emotional struggles await him. Like Tim's relationship with Timmy, my connection to the young David suggests something absolute and unchanging. The bond is energetic, embodied, found in a recognition of life. This recognition, as O'Brien suggests, is not necessarily therapeutic, although some critics understandably want it to be. As Haswell writes of "The Lives of the Dead": "The tale of Timmy is a consolatory one, although this moment of reconciliation seems fragile and precarious. But isn't that because the starting point of healing is the end point of the book?" (101).

If the "tale of Timmy" is consolatory to me, it is because it is a story about a man struggling, through the process of writing, to remain connected to his embodied self. I recognize that struggle and, in turn, feel less alone. Although *The Things They Carried*, as a whole, is about process and not necessarily progress, it does have a certain symmetry. It begins with a soldier trying to acclimate to war ("The Things They Carried") and ends with a former soldier struggling to live with his memories. As to whether "The Lives of the Dead" is "the starting point of healing", I am not inclined to imagine life for Tim beyond the text: the book is what O'Brien gave us. As for O'Brien, I can only look to what he has written about himself or stated in interviews. Almost five years after finishing *The Things They Carried*, O'Brien continued to battle despair, as "The Vietnam in Me" testifies. Ultimately, I find it less interesting to view *The Things They Carried* as a move toward "healing", however the term is understood. The emotional "payoff" is Tim's realization that writing is a means of managing his despair, and that to write is to live; in that way, perhaps, writing has kept him alive through his depressive bouts. This, for me, is sufficient self-knowledge. In her reading of "Lives of the Dead", Chen states: "Return is figured as momentarily possible, a juncture of time, space, and desire that never offers a definitive resting place" (81–82). Recursive and process-oriented, to write is to return, again and again, to the living self. Reading O'Brien, I too return, to ground my orphan pain, find temporary narrative footing, and foster stories of my own.

Works cited

Bates, Milton J. *The Wars We Took to Vietnam: Cultural Conflict and Storytelling.* Berkeley: Calif. UP, 1996. Print.
Carpenter, Lucas. "'It Don't Mean Nothin': Vietnam War Fiction and Postmodernism". *College Literature*, 2003. 30(2): 30–50. *Jstor.* Web. 9 September 2012.
Chambers, Ross. "Orphaned Memories, Phantom Pain: Toward a Hauntology of Discourse". In *Untimely Interventions: AIDS Writing, Testimonial, and the Rhetoric of Haunting.* Ann Arbor: University of Michigan Press, 2004.
Chen, Tina. "'Unraveling the Deeper Meaning': Exile and the Embodied Poetics of Displacement in Tim O'Brien's *The Things They*

Carried". *Contemporary Literature*, Spring 1998. 39(1): 77–98. *Jstor*. Web. 14 September 2012.

Christopher, Renny. *The Vietnam War/The American War Images and Representations in Euro-American and Vietnamese Exile Narratives*. Amherst, MA: Mass. UP, 1995. Print.

Haswell, Janis E. "The Craft of the Short Story in Retelling the Vietnam War: Tim O'Brien's *The Things They Carried*". *South Carolina Review*, 2004. 37(1): 94–109. Print.

Herzog, Tobey C. "Tim O'Brien's 'True Lies' (?)" *Modern Fiction Studies*, Winter 2000. 46(4): 893–916. *Project Muse*. Web. 30 June 2013.

Hutcheon, Linda. *A Poetics of Postmodernism: History, Theory, Fiction*. New York: Routledge, 1988. Print.

Jarraway, David R. "'Excremental Assault' in Tim O'Brien: Trauma and Recovery in Vietnam War Literature". *Modern Fiction Studies*, 1998. 44(3): 695–711. *Project Muse*. Web. 30 June 2013.

Jameson, Fredric. *Postmodernism, or, the Cultural Logic of Late Capitalism*. Durham: Duke UP, 1991. Print.

Kaplan, Steven. "The Undying Uncertainty of the Narrator in Tim O'Brien's *The Things They Carried*." *Critique*, Fall 1993. 35(1): 43–52. Print.

Kaufmann, Michael. "The Solace of Bad Form: Tim O'Brien's Postmodernist Revisions of Vietnam in 'Speaking of Courage'". *Critique*, Summer 2005 46(4): 333–343.Print.

Loeb, Jeff. "Childhood's End: Self Recovery in the Autobiography of the Vietnam War *American Studies*, Spring 1996. 37(1): 95–116. *Jstor*. 30 June 2013.

Martin, Andrew. *Receptions of War: Vietnam in American Culture*. Norman: Oklahoma UP, 1993. Print.

Neilson, Jim. "The Truth in *Things*: Personal Trauma as Historical Amnesia in *The Things They Carried*". victorian.fortunecity.com. 21 May 2001. Web. 14 March 2012.

O'Brien, Tim. "The Vietnam in Me". *The New York Times Magazine*. 2 October 1994: 48–57.

———. *The Things They Carried*. Boston: Houghton Mifflin, 1990. Print.

———. *Going After Cacciato*. New York: Delacorte Press/Seymour Lawrence, 1978. Print.

———. *Northern Lights*. New York: Delacorte Press/Seymour Lawrence, 1975. Print.

———. *If I Die in a Combat Zone Box Me Up & Ship Me Home*. New York: Delta/Seymour Lawrence, 1969. Print.

Scarry, Elaine. *The Body in Pain: The Making and Unmaking of the World*. London: Oxford UP, 1987. Print.

Schroeder, Eric James. "The Past and the Possible: Tim O'Brien's Dialectic of Memory and Imagination". *Search and Clear: Critical Responses to Selected Literature and Films of the Vietnam War*. Bowling Green: Ohio, 1988. Print.

Silbergleid, Robin. "Making Things Present: Tim O'Brien's Autobiographical Metafiction". *Contemporary Literature*, Spring 2009. 50(1): 129–155. *Project Muse*. Web. 30 June 2013.

Waugh, Patricia. *Metafiction: The Theory and Practice of Self-Conscious*. London: Routledge, 1984. Print.

Wilkomirski, Binjamin. *Fragments: Memories of a Wartime Childhood*. New York: Schocken Books, 1996. Print.

8

"The Incessant Rise and Fall and Fall and Rise": Virginia Woolf Treading the Waves

Jessica De Santa

Abstract: *In this chapter, DeSanta explores the aesthetic implications and textual manifestations of Woolf's affective illness as revealed in the essay "On Being Ill" (1930), in which Woolf took on the challenge of "inventing" a language of illness in the distinctive poetics of her fiction, in the absence of an established literary language to communicate the altered body. The vast and varied tumult of Woolf's affective experience translates into a powerful new language of mind and body, informing and transforming her fiction (specifically Mrs Dalloway (1925) and The Waves (1931). DeSanta does not offer a psychoanalytical reading of Woolf, but rather a critical consideration of Woolf's own perceptions of writing and the creative, sensual body, unpacking connections between writing and brain states of affective illness.*

Keywords: Virginia Woolf; affective disorder; poetics; fiction; the altered body

Horton, Stephanie Stone, ed. *Affective Disorder and the Writing Life: The Melancholic Muse.* Basingstoke: Palgrave Macmillan, 2014. DOI: 10.1057/9781137381668.

> Never was anyone so tossed up and down by the body as I am, I think.
>
> *The Diary of Virginia Woolf*, 11 February 1928
>
> Yes, this is the eternal renewal, the incessant rise and fall and fall and rise again. And in me too the wave rises.
>
> *The Waves*, 1931

This chapter explores the esthetic implications of Virginia Woolf's affective illness as disclosed by Woolf in her essay, "On Being Ill" (1930), and as arguably manifest in her novels *Mrs Dalloway* (1925) and *The Waves* (1931). Spurred by Woolf's assertion in "On Being Ill" that illness is a stranger to fiction because there is no established literary language by which to communicate the altered body, I suggest that Woolf invents such a language in her novels. I believe the most illuminative insights into the nature of Woolf's affective illness are not to be found in others' accounts of her condition or behavior, or even necessarily in her own diaries and letters – sources I quote only briefly for context – but in her fiction. To my mind, it is here that she transliterates the vast and varied tumult of her experiences into a powerful new language of the body and senses, allowing the illness in her mind and body to inform, and transform, her prose. Whereas others have provided psychoanalytical readings of Woolf, I offer a strictly critical consideration of her work, in which I focus on her own perceived connections between writing and the creative, sensual body. Beyond reviewing the actual swings and symptoms Woolf recorded, I do not provide fresh clinical insight into her condition.

Much of Woolf's fiction is suffused by a polar tension between opposing psychic states – on the one hand, a mobilizing urge to harness the anarchic sensations and impulses of the body by crafting it into unity with words; on the other, a temptation to surrender to the desires of the body and relinquish language completely. To my mind, these dual and often dueling energies come powerfully to fruition in *Mrs Dalloway* and *The Waves* – only two instructive examples among the full range of Woolf's novels – in which her characters crest and trough precariously upon this ontological and creative problem. Woolf records: "Never was anyone so tossed up and down by the body as I am" (*Diary* 121). I suggest that the episodes that tossed Woolf upon "the waves" both inform the "ups" and "downs" of her fiction and infuse its prose with a closely

DOI: 10.1057/9781137381668

approximated language of the affected body. Here, most evidently, Woolf succeeds in centralizing illness as a literary – or, in her own words, a "poetic" – subject.

Although reticent to name Woolf's "illness" as such, biographer Hermione Lee maintains that Woolf's experiences resemble what is variously referred to as "manic–depressive illness", "bipolar affective disorder", or (more recently) "bipolar disorder", and "cyclothymia", a milder manifestation of bipolar disorder (172). Thomas Caramagno claims that Woolf's symptoms "fulfill the manic–depressive paradigm" (2), and Leonard Woolf similarly referred to his wife as "manic depressive" (176), providing the following account of her symptoms:

> In the manic stage she was extremely excited; the mind raced; she talked volubly and, at the height of the attack, incoherently; she had delusions and heard voices... she was violent with her nurses.... During the depressive stage all her thoughts and emotions were the exact opposite of what they had been in the manic stage. She was in the depths of melancholia and despair; she scarcely spoke; refused to eat; refused to believe that she was ill and insisted that her condition was due to her own guilt; at the height of this stage she tried to commit suicide. (76–77)

At 59, facing the onset of another gruesome period of illness, Woolf did commit suicide by walking into the River Ouse. But Woolf's reflection below, though resonant in aspects with Leonard's account of her bipolar behavior, also reveals a profound life force in her illness – an important connection between the violent seesaw of her body and her creative energies:

> If I could stay in bed another fortnight... I believe I should see the whole of *The Waves*... I believe these illnesses are in my case – how shall I express it? – partly mystical. Something happens in my mind. It refuses to go on registering impressions. It shuts itself up. It becomes chrysalis. I lie quite torpid, often with acute physical pain.... Then suddenly something springs... a tremendous sense of life beginning; mixed with that emotion which is the essence of my feeling, but escapes description... I am swimming in the head and write rather to stabilise myself than to make a correct statement... I then begin to make up my story whatever it is; ideas rush in me; often though this is before I can control my mind or pen. (*Diary* 150–151)

That Woolf's mind "refuses to go on registering impressions", "shuts itself up", and "becomes chrysalis" resembles Leonard's report of her "depressive stage"; the subsequent phase in which "something springs" and "ideas rush" appears to signal a transition to the "manic". Notably, Woolf's tone in this instance is far from suicidal; on the contrary, it is full of wonder as she stands in apparent awe of her body's "mystical" capacities. It appears that the "emotion", which materializes during periods of convalescence, and "which is the essence of my feeling", provides the raw fodder for the "stabilizing" work of Woolf's narrative-spinning: "I believe I should see the whole of *The Waves*". That "mind" and "pen" are thus linked points to a fruitful association – at best – between her illness and her writing: a conceptualization of her condition as a kind of selfless stillness that precedes a productive excess of sensation, thought, and word.

Woolf opens her essay, "On Being Ill", with the following testimony:

> Considering how common illness is, how tremendous the spiritual change that it brings, how astonishing, when the lights of health go down, the undiscovered countries that are then disclosed... it becomes strange indeed that illness has not taken its place with love and battle and jealousy among the prime themes of literature. (3–4)

In Woolf's most whimsical figurations, "illness" is a transcendental journey to the secret "countries" of the spirit: the ill person imagined as an intrepid explorer, even a time traveler. Her call that illness should stand with "love and battle and jealousy" as an important literary subject proposes a new "hierarchy of the passions" in which "love must be deposed in favor of a temperature of 104" (7–8). It encourages a writing practice that gives voice to the specialized knowledge of the altered mind and body. Woolf maintains, for example, that although lovers might rely upon Shakespeare and Keats to express the mysteries of their own hearts, illness has no mouthpiece in English: "[L]et a sufferer try to describe a pain in his head to a doctor and language at once runs dry. There is nothing ready made for him. He is forced to coin words himself, and, taking his pain in one hand, and a lump of pure sound in the other... so to crush them together that a brand new word in the end drops out" (7). The language Woolf requires, in which "pain" and "pure sound" together breed a "brand new word", is not an objective or empirical discourse, but rather closer to music: a sonic speech whose elusion of denotative meaning might more nearly approximate experiences of illness. Woolf imagines this "new language that we need" as at once "more primitive, more sensual, more obscene" (7–8) – in other words, closer to the body. And it is the sensual body in its capricious passions, both ecstatic and wretched, that informs her language-making project.

To Woolf, the body is not only a "monster" but also a "miracle" (6); that writers and philosophers have passed over its destructive–creative capacities in discussing the more "civilised" and civilizing mind (5) is thought by her a disservice to ill and non-ill persons alike. The following assertion resonates throughout her oeuvre:

> [The mind] cannot separate off from the body like the sheath of a knife or the pod of a pea for a single instant; it must go through the whole unending procession of changes, heat and cold, comfort and discomfort, hunger and satisfaction, health and illness…. But of all this daily drama of the body there is no record…. Those great wars which the body wages with the mind a slave to it, in the solitude of the bedroom against the assault of fever or the oncome of melancholia, are neglected. Nor is the reason far to seek. To look these things squarely in the face would need the courage of a lion tamer; a robust philosophy; a reason rooted in the bowels of the earth. (4–5)

Woolf maintains that the idea of a dissociation between the body and the mind is erroneous as the mind "cannot separate off from the body"; rather, "the creature within" is bound to its complex and inconstant morphology. I suggest that the body features as a kind of main character who reappears across the breadth of Woolf's fiction: or perhaps more accurately, the kaleidoscopic states of the mind as played upon by the body's permutations. Rather than treating the mind and body as autonomously operating entities, Woolf instead depicts a natural symbiosis between their presumed "poles". I suggest that an illuminative reading of Woolf is one that approaches her texts as records of "those great wars which the body wages with the mind a slave to it." Fictional iterations of Woolf's own, ineffable affective experiences (though they are not only this), her novels look her illness "squarely in the face" with the "courage of a lion tamer", providing just such a "robust philosophy" of her often painfully sensate body.

Though purely denotative language cannot give voice to illness, as Woolf regrets, metaphors for the sharpened sensual experiences of illness can in fact lend a kind of "body" to language. This, in turn, might effectually create a "poetic" language of the body:

> In illness words seem to possess a mystic quality. We grasp what is beyond their surface meaning, gather instinctively this, that, and the other – a sound, a colour, here a stress, there a pause – which the poet, knowing words to be meager in comparison with ideas, has strewn about his page to evoke, when collected, a state of mind which neither words can express nor

the reason explain... [I]n illness, with the police off duty, we creep beneath some obscure poems by Mallarmé or Donne, some phrase in Latin or Greek, and the words give out their scent and distil their flavour, and then, if at last we grasp the meaning, it is all the richer for having come to us sensually at first, by way of the palate and the nostril, like some queer odour. (21–22)

In an illustrative metaphor for this "mystic quality" which in illness "words seem to possess", Woolf imagines words as sonic and colored, scented and flavored: a feature of the more body-centered poetry she advocates. To her mind, the "poet" treats words as parts of a whole, the whole being "a state of mind which neither words can express nor the reason explain". Through words, that is, poets aspire to the wordless: to ideas that live large and free prior to becoming bound by language and logic. Woolf maintains that we embrace such "incomprehensibility" more readily in illness than in health, when "meaning has encroached upon sound" and "intelligence domineers over our senses" (21). Arguably, then, the ill writer's heated intimacy with this more dilated language of the senses also has profound implications for the reader, who similarly – imaginatively – becomes "ill" in order to access the writer's text by way of her or his own body. This "richer" reading necessitates a sensual comprehension before an intellectual one, a willingness to read with "palate" and "nostril" before eye and brain.

In Woolf's formulation, then, the "gift" of illness is a sanctioned leave from reason: a giving in to eyeless, yet sharper senses indicative of vast intuitive wisdoms in and of the body. Woolf often writes of vision(s) – as in her below reference to "looking at the sky" – but notably this, too, tends to have less to do with literal eyesight than with a more visceral, perhaps even spiritual capacity: "In illness,... we cease to be soldiers in the army of the upright; we become deserters. They march to battle. We float with the sticks on the stream; helter-skelter with the dead leaves on the lawn, irresponsible and disinterested and able, perhaps for the first time in years, to look round, to look up – to look, for example, at the sky" (11–12). In "floating" rather than "marching", Woolf abandons linear, "military"-style thinking and adopts a more multidirectional and "helter-skelter" thought process. The writing that results is therefore more a register of her impressions than a targeted, plot-based agenda. The freedom to "look round, to look up" in illness is exactly the happy possibility available to her in inventing new forms of fictional language. Acknowledging the havoc such distracted, free-associative thinking would wreak in functional society, Woolf playfully admits, "Pedestrians would be impeded and disconcerted by a public sky-gazer" (13). The question of what distinguishes health from illness, then, amounts to the difference between "prosaic" pedestrians and "poetic" "public sky-gazers": those who subscribe to the status quo in language versus those who color outside the lines in thinking and writing more expansively, to the furthest reaches of the imagination. In the shell-shocked World War I veteran, Septimus Smith – who in the following passage of *Mrs Dalloway* is in fact literally "looking at the sky" – Woolf provides a vivid illustration of the latter.

Septimus' extraordinary reaction to the sight of a skywriting airplane in an opening scene of the novel demonstrates a poetic sensibility that resonates with Woolf's descriptions of her own experiences of creative illness. Perhaps in the case of Septimus, who exhibits many of the symptoms associated with post-traumatic stress disorder (PTSD), the figurative ashes in his mouth are to blame for the fact that he "could not taste, he could not feel" (98). And yet – like Woolf's "ill" or imaginatively ill reader, who experiences poetry with her "palate" – Septimus is able to taste a kind of spiritual sweetness that supersedes any flavor detectable by the human tongue. Furthermore, although texts in plain English appear unintelligible to Septimus, he is able to discern in the skywriter's smoky letters a poetic "supertext":

> So, thought Septimus, looking up, they are signaling to me. Not indeed in actual words; that is, he could not read the language yet; but it was plain enough, this beauty, this exquisite beauty, and tears filled his eyes as he looked at the smoke words languishing and melting in the sky and bestowing upon him in their inexhaustible charity and laughing goodness one shape after another of unimaginable beauty and signaling their intention to provide him, for nothing, for ever, for looking merely, with beauty, more beauty! Tears ran down his cheeks.
> It was toffee; they were advertising toffee... "t... o... f ...". (*Mrs Dalloway* 22)

Septimus' response to the skywriting airplane eludes denotative communication, a process dependent upon the fixed, static, and single meanings of individual words. The sign of the commercial, which literally "signals" to Septimus, is divorced from what it normally signifies; he does not associate the advertisement with food or even with the taste of something sweet, but rather discerns in the ephemeral smoke letters – to him, merely "shapes" – a soulful sweetness that is "inexhaustible", "unimaginable", and eternal. The "languishing and melting" letters, like the shallow promises of advertisements, suggest that the fixity of language (even the alphabet: "t...o...f") is illusive. Septimus sees beyond letters and "actual words" to a profounder "beauty" that escapes language (a beauty so profound, in fact, that the word is repeated five times in the passage above as if to hint at the descriptive inadequacies of English, perhaps of any language), recalling Woolf's desire in "On Being Ill" for a more poetic language of the senses. François Defromont similarly observes that a writing practice with a "strong poetic impact" is one that "reaches a climax in the very process of dissolving the barrier between the signified and the signifier" (122). Like Woolf, she imagines the monolithic meanings of words (for example, "toffee" = candy/sweets) giving way to a more porous flux and flow of language in poetic writing. Once a word is liberated from its single, referential meaning, a dreamlike multiplicity of associations becomes possible: much in the way "toffee", for Septimus, triggers a vision of blissful, untasted sweetness. Septimus' tears evoke clear vision, and even revelation, suggesting that his illness enables him to see through the "dissolving" opacity of normative denotation to a more expansive spectrum of potential poetic meaning.

Julia Kristeva provides a provocative context for considering the relationship between Septimus' illness and his poetic sensibilities, discussing productive linguistic exchange as a process in which the semiotic and the symbolic are necessarily in constant dialog. She characterizes the language of the symbolic order as a "logical, simple, positive, and 'scientific' form of communication, that is stripped of all stylistic, rhythmic and 'poetic' ambiguities"; by contrast, the semiotic encompasses pulsions, drives, intonations, and gestures unsignified by symbolic language (151). Kristeva maintains that semiotic expression often manifests in the relative incoherence of madness and poetry (Marcus 232). Read in this context, the more "ambiguous", semiotic language of Septimus' wayward body and emotions might be said to have fallen out of dialog with the more "scientific" and apparently objective, symbolic language of medicine. Septimus' real war – the fight against his untasting, unfeeling body – does not signify to his doctors, Holmes and Bradshaw, just as the skywriter's letters and message become blurred and ultimately unintelligible to their sane eyes. As a result, Septimus perceives the medical intervention and terminology of his uncomprehending doctors as both violent and violating: "Once you fall, Septimus repeated to himself... Holmes and Bradshaw are on you. They scour the desert. They fly screaming into the wilderness. The rack and the thumbscrew are applied" (109). Septimus experiences his doctors' response to his "fall"

DOI: 10.1057/9781137381668

from the normative discourse of the body as perhaps more punitive and torturous than his illness in and of itself. Chafing against the constraints of diagnostic clinical vocabulary, Septimus requires a poetic space where his body's ever-changing vision eludes petrification in the symbols of written words.

Though the bitterness in his final words is palpable, Septimus' ensuing suicide is also written, in one sense, as an offering: he cries, "I'll give it you!" just before he jumps from a window (168). In a parallel sphere, Clarissa Dalloway cannot "give" her party – that is, she cannot offer herself fully and freely to the moment – until she dies, imaginatively, with Septimus:

> Oh! thought Clarissa, in the middle of my party, here's death, she thought.... He had killed himself – but how? Always her body went through it first, when she was told, suddenly, of an accident; her dress flamed, her body burnt..... So she saw it. But why had he done it? ... A thing there was that mattered; a thing, wreathed about with chatter, defaced, obscured in her own life, let drop every day in corruption, lies, chatter. This he had preserved. Death was defiance. Death was an attempt to communicate ... (207–210)

Clarissa's image of Septimus' death – "so she saw it" – is less visual than visceral: "always her body went through it first, her dress flamed, her body burnt". By contrast to Septimus, Clarissa inhabits her body so completely that she is empathically able to experience his death as her own. I would like to add to John Hawley Roberts' claim that Clarissa and Septimus are "opposite phases of an idea of life" (837) by suggesting that they also reflect inverse aspects of an affective illness that resembles Woolf's accounts of her own condition: Septimus in his body's depressive inability to engage with the present and Clarissa in the mystical abilities her sensual imagination imparts. Woolf interjects Septimus' death "in the middle of" Clarissa's party, her celebration of life; one dissociated from the body and the other inextricably body-centered, the two protagonists' united bipolar consciousness counterbalances the narrative.

The pure "thing" Clarissa sees "wreathed about with chatter" also recalls Septimus' preoccupation with the toffee advertisement and with the falsities of words. Both envision language as a kind of fog surrounding a "centre" – a "thing that mattered" – as the skywriter's smoke letters encircle pure expanses of sky. Septimus "flings" life "away" and Clarissa embraces it; Clarissa's creative actualization – her initiation as an artist of life, as it were – depends upon her vision of what Septimus has achieved in death: that is, "an attempt to communicate". Arguably then, Clarissa's celebration belongs to the absent-minded Septimus, who is finally present at her party. Of writing *Mrs Dalloway*, Woolf records: "it seems to leave me plunged deep in the richest strata of my mind. I can write and write and write now: the happiest feeling in the world" (*Diary* 68). Woolf's own "plunge" in writing is reinstated on the novel's first page: "What a lark! What a plunge!" (*Mrs Dalloway* 1) Clarissa thinks as she opens a window to the June morning. Both Septimus' "fall" and Clarissa's "plunge" can be read as entrances into "the richest strata" of the mind, where the created become creators in their own rights.

The novel concludes: "It is Clarissa…. For there she was" (219). Unlike Clarissa, who "is" – fully and presently – Rhoda in *The Waves* is prepositional: another of Woolf's sky-gazers who, like Septimus, "looks far *away over* our heads, *beyond*" (my emphasis) (113). Rhoda appears less as a fully fleshed-out subject within the narrative than as a modality or directional energy; if Clarissa is anchored in her sensual body, Rhoda is relegated to an ontologically peripatetic life of rootless "floating", reminiscent of Woolf's ill, mutinously non-"marching" subject. She perceives herself a complete non-agent, a mere "cork on a rough sea" or a "ribbon of weed" (86–87). Also recalling Septimus, Rhoda's anarchic sense of self precedes her difficulty with language: "I am to be cast up and down among these men and women, with their twitching faces, with their lying tongues… I am the foam that sweeps and frills the uttermost rims of the rocks with whiteness; I am also a girl, here in this room" (86–87). The paradoxical riddle of "I am the foam" and "I am also a girl" points to Rhoda's essential conflict; in a societal sea of able, functioning bodies, she feels as fragile and insubstantial as the bubbles that "sweep" and "frill", in one sense. In another, her body is cumbersome to her and even overwhelming: "We cluster like maggots on the back of something that will carry us on… we settle down, like walruses stranded on rocks, like heavy bodies incapable of waddling to the sea, hoping for a wave to lift us, but we are too heavy" (133). Perhaps Rhoda's fraught relationship with her body also accounts for the way she recoils at the grotesqueness of speaking and language – at the abject theatricality of the "twitching faces" and "lying tongues" of ordinary "men and women". Lacking predatorial agency, as it were, Rhoda is doomed to torture and ultimately consumption by the monstrous eating, speaking mouths that close in upon her. She is not bolstered but rather choked by her own food and words, perceiving herself "gorged" and tick-like, "torpid" as a slug, less than human. Like untasting Septimus, Rhoda is impotent to derive pleasure from her embodiment.

DOI: 10.1057/9781137381668

Rather, she is painfully impeded in her quest to overcome her pendulous body – at once ponderous and barely perceptible – lacking the vehicle of an expressive language to "lift" her and "carry" her "on".

In Rhoda, Woolf again raises the problem of language for those whose relationship with the body is colored by experiences of affective illness. Rhoda is given no diagnosis in *The Waves*, but her suffering bears a strong resemblance to that of Septimus. And though I do not read suicide in Woolf's fiction as an indicator of affective illness – nor do I glorify it as a "poetic" experience – an additional parallel exists between the two characters in that like Septimus', Rhoda's life concludes in the silence of suicide. The only language discernible to Rhoda is that of music, whose myriad abstract "shapes" – like the letters that signal sweetly to Septimus – allow her to puzzle together her disparate experiences of body and of not-body into a unified consciousness. At the concert hall, for example, she is finally able to "state" – and to taste – as an ontological whole:

> "Like" and "like" and "like" – but what is the thing that lies beneath the semblance of the thing?... [Death] has made me this gift, let me see the thing. There is a square; there is an oblong. The players take the square and place it upon the oblong. They place it very accurately; they make a perfect dwelling-place. Very little is left outside. The structure is now visible; what is inchoate is here stated.... The sweetness of this content overflowing runs down the walls of my mind, and liberates understanding. (134)

Exhausted by the superficiality of simile ("like" and "like" and "like"), Rhoda craves an authentic language for "the thing that lies beneath the semblance of the thing", for the actuality of her own experience. Recalling Woolf's desire for a sonic language of illness, she perceives music as a metaphorical merging of shapes, which, jigsawed together, create a "perfect dwelling-place": a haven where "what is inchoate" is finally "stated", her own dissolute nature given voice. Like Septimus, Rhoda can now effectively taste the sublime, "overflowing" "sweetness" of the language that has eluded her, an embarrassment of "understanding" that pools in potential pages of written text.

Just as Clarissa's corporeal vision of Septimus' death is integral to the life-giving, creative event of her party, Rhoda continues to exist in death as a muse in Bernard's writing life. Arguably, in Bernard – as in Clarissa – Woolf centralizes the imaginatively or empathically (if not literally) ill body as a site of selfless creativity. Bernard does not wish to create a referential or meaningful work, but rather a poetry more faithful to the sensual capacities that allow him actually to feel the experiences of his friends as his own: "Here on my brow is the blow I got when Percival fell. Here on the nape of my neck is the kiss Jinny gave Louis. My eyes fill with Susan's tears. I see far away, quivering like a gold thread, the pillar Rhoda saw, and feel the rush of the wind of her flight when she leapt" (241). With his senses, Bernard is able not only to imagine but also virtually to perceive the pains and desires of his friends. The "blow", the "kiss", the "tears", and especially the wind rush of Rhoda's "leap" are reminiscent of Clarissa's vicarious capacity to feel, with her own empathic body, Septimus' fall. Recalling Woolf's claim in "On Being Ill" that in sickness, "we go down into the pit of death and feel the waters of annihilation close above our heads" (3), in writing, Bernard descends to "depths" which are "tideless" and "immune", void of egotistical passions and of the details of his own name and personality: "Immeasurably receptive, holding everything, trembling with fullness, yet clear, contained – so my being seems... now that he is dead, the man I called 'Bernard', the man who kept a book in his pocket in which he made notes – phrases for the moon, notes of features; how people looked, turned, dropped their cigarette ends" (*The Waves* 243). In his reinvented text, Bernard abandons "notes" and gimmicky "phrases", able to envision momentarily the final story of the body: its inevitable, and ineffable, death. But in another mood, equally integral to the creative process, he relates: "an impulse again runs through us; we rise, we toss back a mane of white spray; we pound the shore; we are not to be confined" (233). As for Woolf in periods of illness, the silent stillness of a feeling of bodily transcendence gives way to the electricity of embodied motion: to a physical "impulse" that floods Bernard's consciousness with language.

In *The Waves*, Bernard toes a line in the sand between a potentially overcoming sense of life without body, on the one hand, and an acute sensual awareness on the other: an exhausted desire to acquiesce to selfless, nameless death versus a defiant urge to muscle on, however painfully, in life and in language. But in the balanced examples of Woolf's poetry, the rhythm of "running", "rising" life necessarily corresponds with its inverse: the silent and beatless, the "tideless" and "immune". Woolf suggests that one of the myriad challenges of writing affective illness – of indeed writing – lies in uniting polar realms of consciousness in language: in making the poles speak to each other, as in Rhoda's square and oblong joined. The wave that "rises" in Bernard, "tosses" its mane, and "pounds the shore" recalls the "wild horse" which, for Rhoda, is "life then to which I am committed" (51). In writing, Bernard is similarly committed. His body is not a choice but a reality; its wavering rhythms can galvanize or defeat, subsume him or bear him onward. As an elderly man, Bernard reflects, "Yes, this is the eternal renewal, the incessant rise and fall and fall and rise again. And in me too the wave rises" (247). In Bernard's writing life, as for many of Woolf's fictional creators, it is less a question of either fighting against or surrendering to the "rise and fall and fall and rise" than of treading it.

Works cited

Caramagno, Thomas C. *The Flight of the Mind: Virginia's Woolf's Art and Manic-Depressive Illness*. Berkeley: California UP, 1992. Print.

Defromont, Françoise. "Metaphorical Thinking and Poetic Writing in Virginia Woolf and Hélène Cixous". *The Body and the Text: Hélène Cixous, Reading and Teaching*. Ed. Helen Wilcox. London: Harvester Wheatsheaf, 1990. 114–124. Print.

Kristeva, Julia. "About Chinese Women". *The Kristeva Reader*. Ed. Toril Moi. Oxford: Blackwell Publishers Ltd., 1986. 138–159. Print.

Lee, Hermione. *Virginia Woolf*. New York: Vintage Books, 1999. Print.

Marcus, Laura. "Woolf's Feminism and Feminism's Woolf". *The Cambridge Companion to Virginia Woolf*. Cambridge: Cambridge UP, 2007. 209–244. Print.

Roberts, John Hawley. "'Vision and Design' in Virginia Woolf". *PMLA* 61.3, 1946. 835–847. *JSTOR*. Web. 11 May 2008.

Woolf, Leonard. *Beginning Again: An Autobiography of the Years 1911-1918*. New York: Harcourt Brace Jovanovich, 1964. Print.

Woolf, Virginia. *Mrs. Dalloway*. London: Everyman's Library, 1993.

——. *The Waves*. Ed. Gillian Beer. Oxford: Oxford University Press, 1998.

——. "On Being Ill". Ashfield: Paris Press, 2002.

——. *A Writer's Diary*. Ed. Leonard Woolf. London: Harvest, 2003.

9

The Fire, the Dark, and the Beautiful Distance

Stephen Newton

Abstract: *"Some days stay with us more than others." In gorgeous writing reminiscent of James Agee, Stephen Newton meditates on memory and emotion through figures like Uncle Harold, for whom marital desertion hastened a first breakdown; a carny, "lean, greasy and grimy, nineteen going on sixty", and the scent of death by drug overdose, "the final remnants of a young factory worker's desperate isolation". In another world, "a light shines from a porch into the backyard", he writes. "You saw this once... but now that moment is long gone... Rolling away toward the distant horizon the present becomes the past, while the past opens up to patiently welcome the present in the beautifssul distance."*

Keywords: Memory; emotion; moments

Horton, Stephanie Stone, ed. *Affective Disorder and the Writing Life: The Melancholic Muse*. Basingstoke: Palgrave Macmillan, 2014. DOI: 10.1057/9781137381668.

Lazarus in the bathtub, 1969

Uncle Harold was a whistler. He was the great-uncle of a friend of mine in high school, and had spent most of his life in and out of mental hospitals. Supposedly, his first breakdown was the result of his young wife leaving him for another man. When I knew him, he would spend his days chain smoking Pall Mall non-filters and drinking steadily. On the days when I would skip school and go to visit him, he would sit in the kitchen and tell stories throughout the afternoon. By evening he was invariably drunk, fading in and out of lucidity, his memories of the distant past beginning to blur with the present. When ghosts from buried years began to crowd too close, all vying for attention, and separating reality from the gibbering shadows got too confusing, Harold would start to bob his head and whistle tunelessly, a turkey-necked, pop-eyed old man accompanying some remote rhythm, a barely accessible part of himself. I was a teenager and he was almost 80, and we would drink and smoke until the whistling took over, until he retreated completely, and the stories stopped.

One story Uncle Harold liked to tell was of a time in the 1930s when he was ice fishing with some cronies on Lake George. They were after Northern Pike, the top of the food chain in Adirondack waters – a fierce, atavistic throwback of a fish, with a long mouth full of shark-like teeth. Pike can get to be between 20 and 30 pounds, and almost the length of a fisherman's outstretched arms. Harold and his buddies had caught four or five lunkers, monstrous beauties that looked more at home in the Mesozoic than the twentieth century, streamlined eating machines that had survived eons of natural selection intact.

The men didn't kill the fish on the ice as they caught them that day; when pike are this big, you need a club or a gun, lest you run the risk of a vicious bite. They just left them flopping around in the snow with panting gills until they froze solid. When it got dark they packed up their gear and frozen fish and headed back to Schenectady, hitting a few bars on the way, with the fish stowed away safely in the trunk of the car. But when they got home, there was a problem – they couldn't clean the pike while they were still frozen solid, and they were too big for the freezer. The fishermen decided to fill a bathtub with lukewarm water, and then gradually thaw the fish until they were soft enough to filet. By this time, the pike had been out of the water for eight hours, maybe longer. They put the frozen Northerns into the tub, stiff as cord-wood, and then settled in drinking and playing cards, a traditional end to a day spent on the North Country ice.

When the sportsmen went in to check on their catch, however, fillet knives in hand, they had a startling, almost surrealistic discovery. The pike were alive. The tub was a bone-white porcelain aquarium packed with slippery, streamlined, whiplash muscle and snapping jaws. I don't recall precisely how they dispatched the fish. Uncle Harold's point in telling the story seemed to be the strangeness of it all, the absolutely weird, unexpected, otherworldly way the fish had survived so long out of water, and the disconcerting yet electrifying shock of this encounter with resurrection in the incongruous setting of a bathtub.

Locals up north call pike "snake fish", and they do have a reptilian aspect, a prehistoric quality that sets them apart. They seem to be a very pure kind of predator, silent and ominous and strange, as alien as anything from Andromeda or Alpha Centauri, with a kind of refined yet savage efficiency in killing, but... well, they still are fish, and one doesn't expect to find that they can go into suspended animation like astronauts in a science fiction novel. How long could these time travelers survive, cryogenically preserved like this? Years, maybe even decades? Is there any known limit to the period of possible reanimation if the conditions are right?

Old Scratch at the fair, 1987

In the late 1980s I lived for a year with a young woman in a small carriage house apartment on the side of a trout stream outside of Saratoga Springs, NY. Early one Saturday morning in July, we drove over to a county fair near the Vermont border. We ate fried dough sprinkled with powdered sugar and sausage and pepper sandwiches, walked through barns of prize livestock, and watched little racing pigs run around a track for their reward of an Oreo cookie.

My girlfriend thought it would be fun to go on a ride. I did not, but I reluctantly agreed. This was in a separate part of the fair, pure carnival, seedy, otherworldly, like crossing over to the island of the bad boys in Disney's Pinocchio. The ride consisted of rickety two-seat carts that went around a track shaped roughly like a warped pie-plate – up and down, around and around, faster and faster. As soon as we were seated, waiting for the ride to start, a stringy, tough looking carny – lean, greasy, and grimy, 19 going on 60 – came over to pull down the safety bar. He then

DOI: 10.1057/9781137381668

pulled out a baggie full of pills, a multicolored pharmaceutical grab-bag of yellow uppers, blue downers, striped wigglers and speckled droolers. This guy had a leering, yellowed, gap-toothed grin and a gaunt, simian face, pasty and cadaverous in the flashing lights, and asked if we wanted to buy any pills for the ride. Oh Boy. Now my life was going to be in the hands of a drug-addled lowlife with a rhododendron-root IQ, who was surely out on parole for some unspeakable crime.

The ride finally started, and immediately I knew why I had not wanted to go. I didn't remotely trust the people who moved from town to town and tightened the nuts and bolts on these things. The pill-pushing cretin was in a little patched together pilot-house with a microphone, and after a couple of times around the track he started speeding up the ride, laughing maniacally into a microphone the whole time. Lights were flashing, heavy-metal music was pounding like a rusty chainsaw cutting through corrugated roofing tin, and we rocketed and rattled around the track pressed with chest-compressing force against the back of our seat. The whole time, the greasy-haired troglodyte was giggling into the booming, over-amplified P.A. like Jack Nicholson on bathtub PCP, and, as completely incomprehensible as it was to me at the time, my companion was having a blast, due in no small part to the pole-axed look on my face. I had gone directly into an episode of "Tales from the Crypt", where, with one of Lucifer's minions at the controls I was starring in a low-rent tabloid version of the "Night on Bald Mountain" segment of Fantasia. Beelzebub, Mephistopheles, Belial, Satan, lord of flies, fallen son of the morning star, the man in black, Old Scratch himself in one of his infinite disguises, was stalking the grounds of the Washington County fair, somewhere in between the racing pigs and sausage sandwiches. I mean, who knew?

All creatures here below, 1973

On an August afternoon in the early 1970s, I was walking with a friend on his parent's farm in the southern Kentucky hills, wandering through high meadows straddling broad ridges overlooking the prime bottom-land of the farm's central valley. It was high summer, hot and hazy, with a warm breeze blowing through the old oaks on the hillsides. The tall, unmown ridge top grasses rustled in dry waves, the faint whispered hissing of feathered tassels, and the trees were luxuriant, breathing bountiful and blessed green in the hot Kentucky wind. It was the kind of day when all the world seems to be ablaze, pulsating with sizzling light, tinged with fire without and within.

But as we approached the crest of one of the hillsides we both caught a whiff of something on the breeze that stopped us like we had walked into a wall. In a way we had, but it was a wall of molecules, infinitesimal airborne particles, microscopic missiles of decay, which we interpreted as smell when we came into contact with them through our olfactory apparatus. It was an unmistakable barrage of intense unpleasantness that hit the sensors in the brain like a fist – pungent, rank, a complex of stale, repulsive fumes that lodged in the nose and throat, coating the lungs and stomach. As we got closer, the stench got worse – a foul, dank mist – until we were holding bandannas over our crinkled faces. It was remarkable to me at the time how far the spraying radiance of putrescence had traveled, how pervasive it was, and how overpowering it was. We had walked at least an eighth of a mile before we found the cow, lying on its back, legs straight up, hugely bloated and black in a small, tree-shaded ravine.

The farm was home to about 600 head of cattle, comprising around 200 breeding cows, a much smaller number of bulls, and about 400 calves which were sold for beef when they grew large enough. It was a good-sized operation, and with these many stock it was nearly impossible to keep track of all the animals all of the time. The stock wandered randomly over the hills, wading into the creeks, seeking out, at different times of the day, the cool dappled shade of the woods, or the warm, unremittingly clear sunshine of the high hillsides. The meadows were dotted with clumps of hardwoods, hollows, and swales washed by the shadows of cumulus clouds, groups of cows trailing across in ancient rhythms, timeless in their continuous present, sinuous and blank in the mercy of their days.

The farm was about 2,000 acres, with plenty of room for roaming, and they lost 4 or 5 head of cattle a year – mainly due to calving problems, but occasionally one would die from disease or from eating a poisonous weed. The stage of decomposition of the cow we had found indicated that this was one of those cases. Carrion feeders, contrary to their reputation, are somewhat discriminating in what they will eat, and the smell of death that was so revoltingly overwhelming to us was just a part of a complex palette of similar scents to the dogs, birds, weasels, rats, and skunks, and they could discern subtle nuances that indicated when the meat was tainted. My friend thought that the risk of contagion for the rest of the herd was not significant enough to call a vet for a post-mortem – this was just part of the rhythm of farm life, the natural cycle.

We left the cow in the ravine, to whatever further putrefaction awaited it, but I could not leave the smell. It hung on like an annoying, trashy song that wouldn't stop playing in my mind, palpable as only the memories of scent can be. Surely I must have smelled death before, out walking in the woods, or by the side of the road, but I did not recall ever experiencing this intense, gut-wrenching miasma of decay. This was a strange, unsettling new experience, perhaps because of the sheer size of the animal and the concurrently high gag factor, but in some other disturbing, inchoate way, it was not new at all. Some inarticulate part of me recognized an ancient presence immediately.

Hard work, 1978

Five years later, I was sitting on the front porch of another friend's apartment in Schenectady, NY, drinking beer, kicking back, a warm Sunday afternoon in early spring far removed from the Kentucky hills. I was hanging out with two guys I had known since high school, Dave and Dale – all of us still young, in our 20s, musicians, disaffected dropouts, heavy drinkers, recreational drug consumers like everybody else I knew, and all rebelling, in varying degrees, against what we perceived the numbing conformity of middle-class existence. We were all dangerously susceptible to the short-term pleasures of the intoxicated life, the seductions of the demimonde, and years later that life (in one way or another) wound up killing both of these friends of mine. At the time, however, we were just sitting on the front porch listening to the stereo through open windows, watching the light in the city fade as we passed the late afternoon and early evening in increasingly tranquilized conditions.

Another fellow named Richard, whom we all had known for years, came walking by, drifting down the sidewalk, apparently in some sort of detached fog. He looked numb, shell-shocked, sleepwalking in daylight, like someone had injected his face with Novocain. Richard had taken a roommate a few weeks before, a young man who was a fellow worker at the GE plant in town, who had just recently broken up with his girlfriend and needed a place to live. They were not close friends, just a couple of guys working in the same shop at the factory who were brought together by convenience.

Richard had left Friday afternoon for the weekend, returning early Sunday morning. As he came into the apartment, he smelled something strong and gamy – unmistakably bad, rotten – in the kitchen. He naturally assumed that there must have been a science project from the bachelor refrigerator – a pot of spaghetti with blue fur, some old cheese erupting in a miniature Vesuvius of penicillin cultures – that had been thrown out in the garbage, so he promptly took the kitchen wastebasket and emptied it outside in the trash can on the porch. His roommate's bedroom was off the kitchen, and as Richard walked by the open door on his way down the hallway, he noticed his boarder was sleeping, curled up, facing away from the door. It had been a long drive home from Vermont, however, so Richard just went to his room and laid down for a nap without giving it a second thought.

Richard awoke a few hours later and the smell was inescapable, stronger than ever. By now, not so tired and groggy from the drive, Richard sensed that something was very wrong, and he knew the pungent fog was not coming from the garbage. He went to the door of his roommate's bedroom, saw him sleeping in the exact same position as he had been in hours before, entered the room, and immediately called the police.

When the ambulance arrived, the paramedics only had to get to the bottom of the stairs before declaring the victim dead. They knew the smell. After Richard had left on Friday his roommate had taken an overdose of pills and had been dead for almost two days. The paramedics took the body away; there was a brief rundown of police formalities, and Richard had been walking the streets for a couple of hours stunned, blindsided by the events of the day, an ambulatory automaton with a 1,000-yard stare, when he happened by our porch.

Richard's roommate had taken an enormous quantity of Quaaludes, and after he lost consciousness (or so, for mercy's sake, we wanted to believe), his stomach had hemorrhaged and he had vomited up what seemed to be a huge amount of blood, a startlingly large pool, really, which by now was a coagulated, crusty, blackish raspberry-red mass spread out over the bedroom floor. Pretty bad. Someone needed to clean it up, and Dave, Dale and I decided that Richard had been through enough for one day.

When we got to the apartment, I, also, recognized the smell immediately. It was precisely the same as the day years before on that light drenched Kentucky hillside. In retrospect it seems obvious: we humans are mammals – essentially the same, in biological terms, as a cow or mouse or woodchuck by the side of the road, and we know that someday we are all going to be roadkill as well. But at this moment it was a kind of awakening, recognition of origin and destination. I most certainly had never smelled a decaying dead person before, and as morbid as I could sometimes be, I doubt whether I had ever really thought much about what one might formally call the odor of cadaverous decomposition, or about its connection with our animal brethren nearest to us on the food chain. I had read accounts of battlefield aftermath and had seen news footage of disaster cleanup crews with face masks, and I was in a Horror/Hard-boiled phase in my recreational reading, but the reality of death had up to this point never connected in any concrete way with the images from books, movies, magazines, and television. How could it have? I had been quite lucky, up to that point, and have been since, more or less.

It took us a few hours to clean up the bedroom, but we got through it. We had to take pails of water and scrub brushes, gradually dissolving the dark island of coagulated blood on the bedroom floor, and then mop up the... well, I don't know what to call it that doesn't sound disrespectful and smart-alecky. We were drinking beer and smoking cigarettes, taking shifts at the work. We were learning some hard things about life that afternoon, but we were also losing something, paying a price for the passage. Even with the windows open the smell was thick, tenacious, awful, something that got to you on a cellular level, and none of us could stay in the room for too long at a time without getting sick.

The final remnants of this young factory worker's desperate isolation were slowly being erased by strangers – three equally young men, mopping up his blood in an anonymous upstairs room filled with the fading afternoon light of a busy city. The dark brownish-red in the buckets and on the floor finally faded to rose, growing ever more pale, as we scrubbed and mopped and then dumped and refilled the buckets, until finally the water was clear, and the floor was clean. I had never met him, and I don't remember his name. When we left, the smell had diminished, but it was still there – faint traces slowly dissipating into the air of the room where he chose to leave the earth. We had been cleaning up the remains of this body as if somehow the work was a gift, but it was only a very small thing, an attempt to put order in the place of awful chaos and loss.

After all hallows, 1984

By the mid-1980s I lived in the southern Adirondacks, in an apartment next door to an old hotel called the Stony Creek Inn, the social hub of "downtown" Stony Creek, NY, a metropolis consisting of two bars and a general store on three of the four corners of a mountain crossroads 12 miles from the next nearest town. I was living with a woman who was one of the owners of the Inn, and spending a lot of time at the bar as a sort of house musician, a sideman guitar player playing with whatever musicians came to town, mainly rootsy blues/country/folk/jazz/honky-tonk/swing/rock and roll music, roughly what the kids today call Americana or "y'allternative". This was part of the same musical ethos – coming, that is, out of the same deep-structure and cultural matrix as Jerry Garcia playing Merle Haggard and Miles Davis songs with The Grateful Dead, Duane Allman mixing John Coltrane and Blind Willie McTell, The Band playing an old Johnny Cash murder mystery tune alongside a surrealistic Dylan lament, Emmylou Harris and Gram Parsons singing songs of heartache and loss by the Louvin Brothers, or Ry Cooder mixing Hawaiian slack-key, Tex-Mex conjunto, delta blues, 1920s jazz, and Bahamian hymns, the sliding heart-string music of the border country, a soundtrack for all the travelers in distant river valleys where cultures meet and refugees follow their hopes and dreams in spite of all that they know about the danger and darkness that might lie ahead.

The inn always had a charged, over-the-top Halloween party, and this year was particularly wild. There were some gruesome costumes, the yearly convocation of walking dead, ghouls, vampires, and space aliens, but others conformed to the lineaments of different portions of the psychic landscape. I won the best costume prize for going in drag, a blonde bombshell shamelessly flirting with the judges of the costume contest – three macho prison guards from downstate who were up for hunting season. There were hours of dancing, mercilessly loud country-rock music, and, at least for this one night, a sort of a Monty Python drag queen version of the usual upper-Hudson, wild frontier, north woods drunken lunacy. I wound up the night swozzled, absolutely trashed, pounding down shots at the bar in my blonde wig, purse, party dress, high heels, and pantyhose, and shooting pool with knee-walking, commode-hugging-drunk, redneck local loggers. Yikes. Call the law.

The night went very late, and the next morning, heading bleary-eyed and wet-brained over to Floyd's, the general store across the four corners from the inn, I was met with a macabre, chilling, hallucinatory sight, as if Toto had pulled the edge of the Wizard's curtain back to reveal not a bumbling, benign charlatan, but a roiling mass of maggots swarming over the taut rictus of Auntie Em's face.

Impaled on a spike on a telephone pole next to the store, smack dab in the center of this sleepy mountain hamlet, was the head of a Scottish longhair steer – horns swept wide, dull eyes staring blank, mouth wide open, black tongue lolling out. Under the head hung a rudely scrawled cardboard sign inscribed with the name of the village nag, a foolish, meddling old woman called Mother Lorraine. She lived a couple of houses down from the store, and had called the State Police the previous Halloween when her house had been egged, plastered, and spattered with paint-digesting yolk and albumen, so this was the retribution of some of the wild boys from the surrounding hills, the young longhaired loggers who dressed in red and black, in flannel, leather, wool, and felt, the lads who rattled into town in Toyota trucks and slouched three-deep at the bar drenched in chainsaw oil, sweat, and sawdust.

I went back across the street to get my camera and took a whole roll of pictures. But as I developed them in the darkroom days later, and the image surfaced in the shimmering liquid, rising in the orange glow of the dim light, unscrolling like a minor fugue, there was a chilling recognition, as if I had participated in some terrible alchemy, some awful conjuring that had summoned this face from limbo. There in the tray was the great archetypal hairy horned face, with absent cloven hooves and tail, a totem for every other piked head that had ever graced the sunrise of an unsuspecting town. Alone in the dark, summoning the unholy from the chemical solutions and film, image and memory fused, calling back a bright Kentucky hillside and an ominously still, quiet bedroom, and a smell I could no more forget, as much as I would've liked to, than Lady Macbeth could wash the spots from her hands.

Deep water

It is impossible to know, finally, just what will happen when long dormant memories are reawakened. The past is a palimpsest of faint erasures. It might recover from its suspended animation as a result of buffeting, scourging, and scouring and then open like a flower, with the sustaining, regenerative, life-giving powers of the lotus; the lone offspring of the turbulent storm, a balanced survivor, paradoxically serene, floating peacefully above the churning currents of the deep water, a radiant product of the roiling consciousness upon which the storm depends.

The recesses of memory may also just perpetually hop around cross-eyed, toothless, and brain-dead, a reanimated corpse laughing mindlessly into an interior microphone plugged directly into the crackling, electric blue recesses of the past, while a hapless fool rattles around and around in persistent circles, pinned to the back of his seat under the flashing lights, surrounded by the chest-compressing crunch of hair-straightening devil music, the smell of approaching rain, and jagged flecks of lightning in the distance.

But there is at least one other possibility to consider among the many that suggest themselves. Cryogenically preserved memories could also come back to life hungry, cold-blooded, and mean, convulsing in violent fits of powerful desire, flailing around like pike awakening from an Adirondack deep freeze. They might thrash against each other's protective scales and slam themselves against the confines of their smooth bone-white enclosure, snapping and tearing at anything in sight with the sharp, perfectly formed teeth of an ancient, experienced predator.

Orchids, feathers, and stars, 2001

Outside the gates of the fair, a car pulls away, disappearing around a bend, into the green of the corn, the barely contained profligate breath of summer. A dust cloud rises faintly and then disappears. The first drops of rain hit the dirt with the smell of ozone, and the rumble of thunder echoes off the distant hills.

You saw this once. You were there and were a part of things. Now that moment is long gone, and remains so until a tiny glimpse, the smallest motion seen out of the corner of your eye brings it back, or begins to, the way that midges and fireflies thicken the fading light, yet are themselves invisible on summer lawns in the dusk. There is a haze on these summer evenings that one cannot ever really see by directly looking, only by glancing sidelong, and then only accidentally.

This is the way glimpses are captured – snared in the net of the past, the mesh that is filled with holes, the quilt of space held together with knots and string, with glaciers, vines, and stone, with orchids, feathers, and stars. This is how silence does the work that the rest of our lives leaves undone. The sidelong glance, the overheard conversation, even the implied threat or the rumor, is full of the space that asks, and then answers, the questions that certainty denies.

Some days stay with us more than others. The forgotten past seems to be always potentially there, however, insistent – even relentless – in announcing the presence of its own conspicuous absence, impinging upon the present, waiting to be called into consciousness. It speaks to us in tongues, in runes, in hieroglyphics and blowing sand, in the language of dreams. We run across dark lawns as the sun is going down, through piles of dry leaves along the side of the road, and stare at clouds scudding across the dark October sky. We save our lives, perhaps, with steps we take that bring us closer to home, movements that approximate prayer. We listen to branches rub together and know we are hearing music that we have heard somewhere before – the familiar scratching and rustling whispers, the distant cracks in the wind. It is the sound of flames in space, the echo of origins and darkness and light, of first separation and overarching unity. Never again will we be a part of the heart of things quite as innocently as in this moment, this gift that floats our feet above the dry grass. A light shines from a porch into the backyard. It's suppertime. In a smoky valley, a freight train, charcoal benediction for the noise of the world, pulls silence from the stars and clouds, leaving spiraling nebulae, curling waves of sparks, trailing from its silver wheels. There is noise in the distant branches, then quiet. Leaves and bark are separated by empty space in the cold night. In the hills of frost and stone rolling away toward the distant horizon the present becomes the past, while the past opens up to patiently welcome the present in the beautiful distance.

Index

academia, 51–4
academic writers, productivity and, 55–68
adjunct faculty, 51–4
Aeschylus, 10, 40–1
aesthetic autobiography, 100, 101–2
affect, 8
affective disorders
see also bipolar disorder; depression
art and, 24–42
creativity and, 82
experience of, 43–54
heredity and, 90–3
impact on families, 90–2
pain caused by, 9
productivity and, 55–68
rhetorical analysis of, 10
treatment for, 60–1
women and, 88–9
writing and, 4–10
alcohol abuse, 89
Alger, Horatio, 63
alienation, 109
altered body, 120, 124–6
Alvarez, A., 38
American values, 62–4
amygdalae, 4
ancestral memory, 31
Andreasen, Nancy, 6–7, 13, 14, 91
antidepressants, 60–1, 67
anxiety, 59
Apollo, 35

appetite-as-archenemy, 10
archetypes, 34
Ariel (Plath), 16–18, 39
Aristotle, 6
art
mental illness and, 8, 24–42
rumination and, 6
as self-expression, 85
artists, as outsiders, 37–40, 41

Bagoley, Lise, 43–54
Bahr, David, 100–15
Ballard, Nancer, 24–42
Bawer, Bruce, 105
Beard, Jeannie Parker, 69–77
Becker, Jillian, 16
Beckett, Samuel, 39
The Bell Jar (Plath), 39
belonging, 37–40
Bergler, Edmond, 10–11
bipolar disorder, 5, 6, 7, 82, 88–9
creativity and, 46
living with, 49–54, 70–7
pain caused by, 84
suicide and, 7
treatment for, 45, 48–51, 89–90
of Virginia Woolf, 116–28
writing and, 94–6
body, 120–1, 124–6, 127
Bolton, 86
Boston Public Library murals, 29–32, 33, 39–40, 41
Bowker, Norman, 108–9

brain, affective networks in, 8–9
Brand, Alice, 13
Braun, Alan, 12

Calvino, Italo, 35
Caramango, Thomas, 118
Chambers, Ross, 105–6
coded language, 72–3
cognitive distortions, 7, 87
combinatory thinking, 14
community, 38
confessional poets, 17
conflict, 32–3
connection, 32, 37
Conrad, Joseph, 10, 12
contextual memory, 30–1
creativity, 25, 26, 40, 46, 66–7, 82, 96
curriculum vitae, 56–7, 64–5, 68
cyclothymia, 92, 93

Darkness Visible (Styron), 6, 63–4
deadlines, 4, 36
death, 58
  control over, 38–9
  preoccupation with, 38, 91
Defromont, François, 123
Deiudicibus, Joann K., 79–99
delusions, 27–8
delusions of grandiosity, 16
depression
  creativity and, 66–7
  definition of, 25
  executive function and, 7
  experience of, 6, 46, 63–4, 81
  poetry and, 16–18
  productivity and, 55–68
  statistics on, 5
  stigma of, 62–3
  thought processes in, 7
  trauma and, 102–3
  treatment for, 67
  women and, 88–9
  writing and, 4–10, 86–7, 93–4, 111–12
De Santa, Jessica, 116–28
despair, 39
diagnosis, 8

Diagnostic and Statistical Manual of Mental Disorders, 25
dialectic method, 69–77
Dickens, Charles, 12–13
Dickey, James, 82, 88
Dickinson, Emily, 14, 80
disabled bodies, 8
disconnection, 32, 37
disease, 62
Doessekker, Bruno, 101, 105–6
drug abuse, 89
Duke, Marshall, 86–7
dysthymia, 102

early-morning awakening, 16–18
Ehrenreich, Barbara, 64
embodied memories, 102–6
Emmons, Kimberly, 10
emotions, 8–9, 129–40
expressional fluency, 14
extraordinary brains, 8

fear, 28
female poets/writers, 79–99
  see also specific writers
  mental illness in, 94
  suicide rates for, 5
Fini, Leonor, 37
Flaherty, Alice, 12, 15
foster writing, 105–6
Foucault, Michel, 4
Frank, Arthur, 62
Franklin, Benjamin, 63
Freud, Sigmund, 13, 16, 34
Frost, Robert, 3

Garland-Thompson, Rosemarie, 8
gender roles, 80
Gombrich, E.H., 85
Goodwin and Jamison,
  Manic-Depressive Illness, 15
grandiosity, 16

hallucinations, 27–8
happening-truth, 103–5
Hashimoto's thyroiditis, 92
Haswell, Janis E., 104, 112

Index

healthy-mindedness, 10
Hendin, Herbert, 91
heredity, 90–3
Hermeticism, 72
Herzog, Tobey, 102, 105
Hesiod, 29
Hippocrates, 9
Hjortshoj, Keith, 11
Homer, 25, 31, 32
Hornbacher, Marya, 82, 84, 88–9, 90, 95
Horton, Stephanie Stone, 2–23
Housman, A. E., 35
Hutcheon, Linda, 102, 103
Huxley, Aldous, 31
hypergraphia, 15
hyperspace, 111
hypomania, 6, 7, 13, 14, 45–7, 89, 93, 95
hypothyroidism, 92–3

illness, 62–3, 117–19, 121
  see also mental illness
insanity, see madness; mental illness
inspiration, 33–6
institutionalization, 82–4
isolation, 93–6

Jack, Jordynn, 9
James, Henry, 13
Jameson, Fredric, 102
Jamison, Kay, 14, 82, 84, 88, 93, 96
Jong, Erica, 87
Jung, Carl Gustav, 34

Kabbalah, 72–3
Kafka, Franz, 80, 87
Kantor, Martin, 11
Kaplan, Steven, 102
Kaufman, James, 8, 88, 94
Kenyon, Jane, 66–7
Kevles, Barbara, 85, 86
Kirsch, Adam, 14
Koestler, Arthur, 34–5
Koy, Sina, 31
Kraepelin, Emil, 14
Kramer, Peter, 15
Kristeva, Julia, 4, 123

language, 72–3, 103, 119–21, 124, 126
  coded, 72–3
  metaphoric, 32–3
  research on, 7
Leader, Rose, 11
Leader, Zachary, 11, 12
Lee, Hermione, 118
Lehrer, Jonah, 5–6
lithium, 15
Live or Die (Sexton), 80, 87–8
living, preoccupation with, 38
Loeb, Jeff, 110
Lorde, Audre, 32, 37
Lowell, Robert, 5, 13, 15, 16
lyricism, 109, 110

madness, 74–7, see mental illness
  divinely inspired, 9–10
  inspiration vs., 34–6
  poetics of, 15–18
  writing about, 82–4
Mallarmé, Stéphane, 11
mania, 6, 7, 88–9
  experience of, 47–8, 70
  increased creative responses to word associations, 7
  writing and, 13–15, 94–5
manic-depression, 5, 6, 7, 9
manic euphoria, 14
Martin, Emily, 8
McClatchy, J.D., 86
McKim, Charles, 30, 31, 33
medications, 15, 48, 50–1, 60–1, 67
melancholy, 6, 16
memory, 11, 27, 30–1, 34, 80–1, 102, 129–40
mental hygiene, 6
mental illness
  see also affective disorders; madness
  art and, 8, 24–42
  cultural meanings of, 62–3
  definition of, 25–6
  disclosure of, 8
  experience of, 25–6
  isolation of, 93–6
  perceptual disturbances in, 27–8

mental illness – *continued*
  stigma of, 62–3
  writing and, 89–90
Menuhin, Hephzibah, 32
meta-fiction, 101, 102–4
metaphors, 32–3
Meyer, Louis, 6
Micciche, Laura, 8
Middlebrook, Diane Wood, 81, 85, 94
Milner, Marion, 28
Milton, John, 16
mood disorders, *see* affective disorders
mood stabilizers, 60–1
mortality, 58
"Mr. Lunatic," 73
Mrs Dalloway (Woolf), 117, 122–7
Muses, 27, 29–30, 32–5, 39–41

Nana-Ama Danquah, Meri, 37
neurodiversity, 54
neuroimaging (PET, SPECT, fMRI), 13
neurorhetorics, 9
neuroscience, 7–8, 9, 12
Newton, Stephen, 129–40
Nietzsche, Friedrich, 3
nightmares, 16–17

Oates, Joyce Carol, 16, 17
O'Brien, Sharon, 55–68
O'Brien, Tim, 100–13
"On Being Ill" (Woolf), 116–28
O'Neill, Eugene, 39
optimism, 64
Orne, Martin, 80–1, 83, 85, 89
orphaned memories, 105–6, 107
orphaned pain, 100, 107–9, 113
Orpheus, 40
Ozick, Cynthia, 32

painters, 28
panic attacks, 92
perceptual disturbances, 27–8
personality change, 44
personality traits, 90–1
Phaedrus (Plato), 9, 34
phantom pain, 100, 105–6, 107, 109
Plath, Sylvia, 5, 13–18, 39

Plato, 9, 10, 34
poetics, 15–18, 118
poetry, 14–18, 96
poets, 86, *see* also *specific poets*
  confessional, 17
  female, 5, 94
  manic-depression in, 15
  Romantic, 34
  suicide rates for, 5
postmodernism, 101–4
post-traumatic stress disorder (PTSD), 122
prefrontal cortex, 12
"present past," 102, 103–4, 107–8
productivity, 55–68, 94
Pryal, Katie Rose Guest, 8
psychiatry, 9
psychosis, 47
publication pressure, 55–68
puns, 14
Puvis de Chavannes, Pierre, 30–3, 41

rational though, 34–5
reason, 8
rehappening, 107–8
The Republic (Plato), 9
rhetoric, of neuroscience, 9
rhetorical strategies, 8
rhyme, 14
Roberts, John Hawley, 124
Romantic poets, 34
Rose, Katie, 8, 12
rumination, 5, 6, 93–4
Ruskin, John, 14

Scarry, Elaine, 110
schizophrenia, 6–7, 27, 101
self-censorship, 12
self-medication, 70
senses, heightened, 14, 17–18, 28
sensory experience, 28
sensory memories, 30
Sexton, Anne, 17, 80–92, 94, 96
Sexton, Jenal, 88
Sexton, Linda Gray, 81, 82, 90–2
Slater, Lauren, 8
sleep deprivation, 50

social media, 72, 73
Socrates, 9–10
Socratic dialogue, 69–77
Solomon, Alexander, 25
Sontag, Susan, 10, 62
sound association, 14
stigma, 62–3, 82
Stirman and Pennebacker studies, 7
storytelling, 106, 107–8, 110–11
story-truth, 103, 104, 105
Styron, William, 6, 55, 63–4
subjectivity, 104
substance abuse, 89
suicidal ideation, 38–9, 111
suicide
   bipolar disorder and, 7, 18, 84
   of Plath, 16
   of Sexton, 90–1
   of Woolf, 118
   writing and, 86–7
suicide rates, in writers, 5

Tchaikovsky, Peter, 35
Tharp, Twyla, 26, 28, 32
Theogony (Hesiod), 29
The Things They Carried (O'Brien), 100–13
   as aesthetic autobiography, 101–2
   "Good Form," 104–6
   "How to Tell a True War Story," 106–8
   as meta-fiction, 102–4
   "Notes," 108–9, 110
   "Speaking of Courage," 108–10
   "The Lives of the Dead," 110–11, 112–13
   "The Vietnam in Me," 111–12, 113
   writing style of, 104–13
Thomas, Katherine, 86–7
time, 66
To Bedlam and Part Way Back (Sexton), 82–4, 87
traumatic events, 102–3
treatment, 45, 48–51, 67, 83, 84, 89–90
truth, 103, 105, 107

unconscious, 26, 35, 85–7
unipolar depression, 5

unknown, 26
upward mobility, 63, 64

Van Gogh, 13, 14
Vatz, Richard, 9
Vietnam War, 101, 103

Waugh, Patricia, 103
The Waves (Woolf), 117, 119, 126–8
Wedding, David, 87
Weldon, Fay, 38
Welty, Eudora, 38
Whitman, Walt, 15
wholeness, 40–1
Whybrow, Peter C., 89, 95–6
Wilkomirski, Binjamin, 105–6
women, 88–9
Woolf, Virginia, 10, 14–15, 25, 116–28
word association, 14
work ethic, 63
World Health Organization (WHO), 5
worry, 57
writers
   being a writer, 73–4
   female, 79–99
   "mad," 8
   as outsiders, 37–40, 41
   preoccupaton with life and death by, 38–9
   suicide rates in, 5
writer's block, 10–13, 67–8, 94
writing
   bipolar disorder and, 94–6
   depression and, 4–10, 82, 86–7, 93–4, 111–12
   experience of, 3–4
   foster, 105–6
   isolation of, 93–6
   mania and, 13–15, 94–5
   mental illness and, 89–90
   process, 86
   research on, 7–8, 12
   schizophrenia and, 6–7
writing life, 73–4
writing productivity, 55–68, 94

Lightning Source UK Ltd.
Milton Keynes UK
UKOW04n1356110214

226268UK00001B/13/P